Contents:

THE RAIN AND THE FLIES
two novelettes, one volume

THE RAIN

OPENING STATEMENT

My name is Ryan Elliott-Walker. I am 18 years of age. I am alone, and I am alive. I live in a city called Wakefield—heartland of West Yorkshire, Northern England—and up until The Rain came, I lived here, quite happily, with my dad and our dog. I am starting this journal, today, on the 9th of March to record my experiences here on out and to recount in detail the precession of maddening events thus far I have witnessed. Earth, as it was known, has fallen. A dark and ulterior mind possesses the living. Civilisation has turned viciously upon itself, deranged and unresponsive. There are few left with sane and bearable countenance, and of the few left, there are no youth; all younger than myself disappeared from the Earth, the day The Rain came (I saw it happen, the children disappear! Not a single other soul than myself seemed to realise, when every child and toddler and newborn were beamed into the sky by flying, green saucers. That's right, I said *flying, green saucers*.)

I lived with a silent fear long before all of this happened,—a fear that one day everything was going to fall apart in the blink of an eye, in the time it takes to step on a sand castle. All I can feel there is left to do now, other than survive and search for those not yet unmistakably mad, is write, and try to stay sane in and of myself. I will record what it is I have thus far seen, and shall continue to do so until either the blood in my veins dries up or I am murdered.

From one of few stable minds left to wander the face of the Earth, here is *The Rain*.

FEBRUARY 23RD, FIRST RAIN

There were no clear signs, no broadcasting by news stations of to the medium that would destruct us, no word in the streets, (no one could have really seen it coming). It was sudden. And I'll admit, I, too, was oblivious to by what means 'the end' would arrive. There was one sign, however, and a rather landmark omen too.

Birds, bit by bit, had disappeared from the skies. Cats had vanished, left their homes and not returned. Not one cat had prowled the streets for mice, not one mouse the streets, not even one bird eventually could be seen flying overhead or swooping or landing anywhere insight. Not any critter of any sort, on legs or slithering or with wings, remained in the open to be seen. Hamsters and gerbils, lizards and geckos, had clawed and scratched until bloody their cage walls to be found the next day dead, grieved momentarily by owners. Parrots and budgies kept as pets, too, had gone wild in their cages, until desperate owners came to no other choice than but to let them loose, and they flew away, briefly their colourful feathers seen flying through the empty, silent skies of unsure and frightened neighbourhoods.

The only animals to have stayed loyal were the dogs, and even at that, there had been a dramatic rise in dog attacks. Loved canines turning on their owners, stark wild, unhinged. The news reported a string of the attacks, blindly leading up to the event I am about to entail. It was deemed 'A coincidental psychological breakdown in animals otherwise stable and harmless.' The rest, the disappearances, lead to many 'doomsday' theories,—but when isn't there a crackpot, like myself you might once have thought had you known me before, raving on in quiet corners about the end of times? No one took note, (yet each man, woman, young-man and young-woman grew with a hidden, inner mount of tension that toward the end I had never felt so at peace; for I wasn't alone, I wasn't hiding my fear anymore—everybody else was).

The last news report I ever saw: news presenters accompanied by guest doctors rambling on about how there is no need to panic, that a new form of rabies had not hit the streets, that there is ultimately 'nothing to worry about', attempting then to summarise the disappearing, mass migration and the frenzy of caged animals to be but their sensitive reaction to the poles of the earth having shifted; the last fear of humanity hushed through the magic box, the *tele-hypno-vision*, whilst we all sat on our backsides oblivious to the real threat and its inescapable medium, to the tyranny the weather that afternoon would play, and the static that would then fill our screens forevermore.

It was two weeks ago. It was the day the psyche of every individual was turned inside-out. It was the day the carnal nature within became a monotonous, tone-deaf predominance over the decaying wit and moral esteem of we, O' Humanity. It was the day everyone stopped living. I call it The Reckoning of Greed, The Rapture-less End, Armageddon's Lust—or, more simply, *The Rain*. It was a Sunday, the twenty-third of February, and not a single person outside of myself did I encounter with the sanity to watch the sun go down.

I was walking my dog Rocky, a Staffordshire Terrier, when she went wild. I hadn't expected it. Yeah, sure, it was all over the news at the time: Be careful of pets; Look for suspicious signs; Report anything unsettling to the local impound or authorities. But she'd given me no real worry... apart from her dreams. They'd taken a rough turn a few days back, and sleep seemed to be all she could get. She'd growled for hours on end while she slept, even snapping her jaws, and with such vehement, but I figured it was the atmosphere of late, you know... animals sense things we don't, even if they can't watch the news channels and understand things on a level with us; animals sense when the world is on the brink of collision, when the tides of harmony suddenly ripple.

Anyway, we were walking through the woods around a large lake about two miles back from my home, when she stopped still. Dead still. She wouldn't move.

Her ears perked. Her eyes beamed ahead, stuck on something, startled, shivering in their sockets. Then she was off, howling and bounding like a crazed bull, after some red 'X' in the unseeable distance. I chased her down, calling her name over and over. I carried on and the woods thickened around me.... She'd taken us off the beaten track and I was quickly beginning to feel irrevocably lost, her howling now faint and mocking from every far corner.

I quickly didn't know where I was,—though, of course, I knew my way back, as I hadn't made a turn.

The light had grown thin rapidly, trees disallowing it, and she was nowhere in sight as I jogged on breathless and then tripped and fell over her! Out of nowhere, she'd appeared directly in front of me. I fell hard and tumbled.

I sat up and she came to me. Her tail wagging. Her tongue lolling. I'd been running and raving aloud, bounding through the density of a forest I had never ventured the depth of. "And for what?" I asked her, scornfully.

I felt as a lunatic; my sanity mocked me: for eyes stared at me everywhere. The dark of the wood was lined with them. Eyes, wide, watching, feral.

The forest slowly awoke with the murmur of disturbed creatures. Masses of birds shot from the branches of trees, tweeting sharply. Rocky began to growl. Hissing emerged around us. The eyes pressed in, and then out of a blur of darkness ahead stalked several foxes, dogs, cats, and a horse. I didn't have time to register all the species setting upon us out dark thickets, as the horse neighed and reared and frightfully I, on my feet, spun around to flee.

The faces of cats became clear up from within the branches of trees, their fangs poised in my direction as I ran. Owls hooted hysterically amongst the tweeting of birds; a mad flapping of wings beating loudly in the hanging dark. Gushes of wind flurried around me as birds swooped and weaved in the air. Thankfully, Rocky had listened when I had bolted and called her name. I could hear her snapping at the air as I'd started to run, and I didn't know at first if I was leaving her behind or not; and then, as I called to her, she came obediently to my side.

Thoughts spread through my brain like wildfire as I fled the scene. What had just happened? The animals hadn't wanted me there. They were hiding... but from what? us? ...Humans?

And like clockwork to my discovery, The Rain began.

There had been no warnings. There had been signs, apparently; the animals, the disappearances. But no one, not even the animals, I'm sure, were aware by what medium the fall of mankind was to come—or what would follow.

A smell like rotting flesh descended upon us. Rocky began to whimper. *Rain*, out of nowhere, from a cloudless sky, hit me in the face. And I mean *hit*. It was torrential. Instantly. And it was red, a chemical red. It stung my eyes and distorted my vision.

We needed shelter, fast. The once thick cover of trees had shrunk as we fled the dark depth of the woodland. We but ran, on and on. Rocky didn't leave my side, in the grip of wild panic as we were. I stooped down and picked her up. The Rain, blinding my senses, painted everything a thick, delirious blood-red. I knew there was a sheltered bench nearby but I couldn't see, couldn't make anything out clearly for the fucking-colour-red!

I stumbled with Rocky in my arms, her fur drenched and sticky, her muscles and limbs convulsing.

All I could hear was The Rain crashing to the earth around me—that and Rocky's whimpers, just surfacing through the total chaos.

I didn't find the shelter I knew was close by. Instead, I slipped, stumbled, slipped again and again, and then came crashing to the ground where I chose to lay still and wait, with utter hopelessness like stones in my gut, for The Rain to end.

My arms were wrapped around Rocky tightly. I didn't let go of her. Even when her whimpers reached such a horrendous screeching and she struggled so badly to escape me that I knew I was hurting her, I didn't let go. I didn't want her to run off, blinded in all this red rain falling from the sky, to stumble and slide dangerously through the wake of The Rain as it proceeded to crash down upon us. And then came the smell again. Death and decay. It was in my nostrils and I wanted to vomit before I had physically breathed its toxins in. My stomach tightened with an awful feeling and my throat filled with sick. I laid there like this, spewing my last meal up, drenched in a slimy, sticky, red liquid, cold and terrified, until The Rain stopped and all that was left was an evaporating red mist and that vile, vile smell.

THE NEXT FEW HOURS

Upon my arrival home I immediately ran the shower and climbed in with Rocky. Her fur was sticky and clumped together. The hot water rinsed off the residue of The Rain from my skin and hair, but the smell had clung heavily to my clothes—which wasn't a problem, as I had just thrown them into the bin out back before coming indoors—they were just clothes, after all. Rocky's fur was another issue, however.

I had to bathe her several times. And even when all the stickiness and the red stains had been washed out, the smell was still there. She whimpered quietly as I scrubbed and scrubbed. She was always fine with baths, had never cried once before. The reason she was crying now? Maybe the smell. Maybe what had just happened couldn't register with her and she was still terribly afraid. Maybe I was scrubbing too hard.

I managed to cover the smell with scented gels to the point that you could only sniff the rotten reek ever-so-slightly and only when you got close enough to her fur that it hit you. Her hide still shivering, I carried her downstairs and put her on a couch in the conservatory at the back of our house.

I can't remember a great deal of our walk home. I ran most of the way, and a strange sickness seemed to be swaying in my head.

When The Rain had stopped, I immediately clambered to my feet and pulled Rocky with me. Visibility wasn't too great. There was a mist. A red haze in the air. That *smell*, too. I had to walk quarter of the way home until it finally began to clear enough for me to safely jog and without slipping into things I couldn't see! And even then, as I stood there in my conservatory, my terrified and clean dog shivering behind me on a couch, I could still see a slight tinge of red discolouring the world outside.

I still, to this day, two weeks later, have no real inclination to what or where that rain came from. But what it did, however, became apparent over the next few hours.

Car tyres came rolling into the drive. I heard my father's car door slam shut, followed by ungainly, quick steps. The back gate opened, and there he was, my father, but he wasn't wet, drenched like I and Rocky had been, when he walked into the back garden and view of the conservatory. He wasn't soaked in the red slime of that horrid rain, didn't appear sticky, or unhinged, frantic, as I and Rocky had felt. But when he opened the conservatory door and walked inside, he had this peculiar look in his eyes. "Dad?" I remember saying, but he didn't answer. He just walked straight into the house, his eyes shivering us a brief glance.

I sat down next to Rocky and began to stroke her fur. I felt nervous and Rocky only made me feel worse. I sat there to stroke her fur and she flinched beneath my fingers, her head jerking away in quiet whimpers. When I looked at her, she was sleeping. Her eyelids shut, her breathing quick and shallow. She seemed horrified within her sleep. I withdrew my hand and sniffed my palm: a floral fragrance. I stood up and walked into the kitchen.

My father was in the living room when I found him. The kitchen was littered with his clothes. The *smell* was faintly on them, in the air, faintly. I walked around the kitchen, picked all his clothes to throw in the bin outback; for, sniffing them, they were ruined with that smell, clinging to the fabrics,—yet not drenched, no slime or stickiness, not even a dampness was to them.

I didn't think he'd want them anymore, and I thought, at first, that he would be upstairs in the shower trying to clean his hair and skin of that permeating smell. So I flicked on the kettle and watched the sky slowly filling with clouds from the kitchen window. The mist had completely gone, as far as I could see, and dark clouds scattered the sky. In fact, it was raining slightly, as I remember, a normal clear rain. There wasn't any sign of a red tinge, no discolouring to the clear droplets that were now falling from the clouded sky. I'd have thought myself completely mad at this point if it wasn't for the fact that my father's clothes had been sprawled, or thrown, across the kitchen floor, containing the smell I'd spent at least half an hour scrubbing from my dog's fur. And then the living room door *clicked* open and a gap of noise and darkness peeked into the kitchen.

"Dad?" I asked, like I had before. The living room was in total darkness except for a slight glow. When I opened the door I saw that the television was turned on and the blinds were closed. The noise of static filled the room with a constant buzz, and in the dim light beaming from the television, my father's figure could be made out to be twitching, his right arm spasming, rapidly, in the dark.

I switched on the light. And there he was. Naked. Eyes transfixed on the television screen. His face a blend of anger and frantic, lustful emotion, his mouth smiling crookedly. His arm however wasn't spasming. He was jerking off. "Dad!" I shouted.

He sighted me, peripherally, from the corners of his eyes. "Get out! Turn off the light!" he spat and hissed.

I hit the light switch and closed the door. I couldn't believe what I'd seen. Naked and masturbating! That *look* over his face,—the contorted expression; the sound and quality of his voice. At this point, I couldn't handle my mind, The Rain, the absolute lunacy. I sat on my dog's couch in the conservatory where I remained for the next few hours. I watched the world as it began to rain harder and harder outside. I was a wreck, and the rain, well, the clear, normal rain calmed me as I watched it pour and pour over the conservatory in hard waves and pelts; I felt as though all the madness of the previous few hours were being slowly washed away by the clear rain, and I closed my eyes.

It was dark out when I next opened them.

#

Rocky was still asleep, her head quivering upon my lap, and the day had turned to night, when I awoke. Darkness filled the skyline and not a single light could be seen in the streets. Not a single street lamp had turned on. Which was queer, because I thought, to myself, that they all came on automatically, and the electrics were working in my home…. I had also thought that rain came from clouds and not open skies.

When I went into the living room, there my father still was. He had passed out. And the colour red, like the liquid which had been at the start of this chaos and confusion, covered his legs and his groin. Red hand prints had dried on his stomach and the couch in large smears. I caught a regrettable glance at the centre of it all and saw his inflamed, torn penis limp between his legs—

the source of his blood about him. He'd sat there, deranged, staring at the blank fuzz of static greys and blacks from the television screen, masturbating until he had chaffed away the skin of and ruptured his male member.

I ran upstairs and grabbed his bed quilt. He looked pale. He looked so ill. I couldn't do much for him. I just covered him up with his quilt and brought a glass of water. At first I was going to wake him and offer the drink, but then I just threw the liquid at him. He didn't stir, his face pale and clammy to touch, his breaths shallow, his eyelids heavy and purple. He didn't wake, didn't move, didn't show a sign of life past that of the slow rising of his chest. At least he's not dead, I thought.

Once I'd turned off the television, I tried to wake him, and several times. He was alive; I felt for a heartbeat; and, now and then, when he took in breaths, strangely, he would twinge, as though his body *wanted* to wake.

The phone lines weren't operating when I checked for a dial tone. Like, I'm still afraid to consider this the *whole truth*, but it was like the entire world had just stopped living, simultaneously. No streetlights. No signal. The television static; the phone lines....

I saw my father's keys on the computer desk to his right. I picked them up with the intention of driving to my mother's where she and my eldest brother lived. I didn't know if the roads would be chaos or if they'd be dead; either littered with unmoved vehicles or vehicles unable to move for congestion;—or as dead as the grave, absent both vehicles and persons.

I checked on Rocky. She was asleep still. Quivering less. She looked okay. I had hope that she might be awake, even happy, when I arrived back home with my eldest brother and our mother onboard… my mission…. My *mission*, I remember thinking at this point, how utterly absurd; I'd gone for a walk, my dad wasn't supposed to be home until the next morning from work. I forgot poo bags for Rocky. She wasn't supposed to go until the woods.

I'd cry to these blank pages now as I fill them, but the world since this point has for the moment riddled me of any explorable emotion, numbed my heart, and placed a churning *sickness*, never-ending pain of sorts, in my stomach, every morning to that I awake….

I should be doing more for my dad, and urgently, I remember thinking.

My father's actions and countenance, the quality of his communication, were too grand an horrible thrall over my neurones, I believe, after that point, my mind was thrown like a wrench from the cogs of panic into the cogs of sheer dismay that I had seemingly forgotten that, at the time of and leading up to my father's self-exposure, he had most likely been *infected* with some kind of pathogen that had systematically inhibited and possessed his functioning,—that he had been REDUCED to the madness which possessed him!, and that he needed help. Medical attention. *What if he bleeds out?* I thought, and, without further distraction, I acted in his best interest.

When next I looked at him, sat slumped on the back seats of our navy-blue Rover 45., where I had placed him, his blood had soaked the quilt I'd wrapped him in and was creating dark prints where he sit.

He had been as heavy as a corpse when I'd carried him to the car. I felt so drained, my chest and stomach a hollow cave, as I pulled out of the drive and set off for the nearest hospital in darkness, my limbs profusely shuddering, my will very much overcome by a weakness and great fear.

The roads were dead like the grave. No cars. No persons. I quickly made it to the hospital on the other side of town, racing, my headlights shinning like jousting sticks through the dark—the only source of light to be seen but for the odd streetlamp I found strangely lighting my way (as though by some miracle or coincidence, so that I would not get lost).

I flew into the hospital carpark and found it full, and then, too, I found the hospital full and crowded with people following that. At first, with the carpark and all the cars still there, I had a great swell of hope overwhelm me.

I took the torch my father kept inside his glove compartment, and I made to head through the front entrance of the hospital. Inside, half the lights were still on, mostly just near the entrance, but others, too, oddly scattered about, lit dark spots in a but mostly consuming, indoor darkness. I paused as I entered; I could hear faint noises, faint but *repetitive* sounds, further inside, echoing around the building. And I knew, somewhat instinctively, that all I would find would be strange happenings; the sounds, you see, were like the kind associated with a constant itch, and they were intertwined with small grunts and moans flung through the air to bounce off unsuspecting walls, finding my ears from all sides!

With my father's actions earlier that evening still in my mind, I shouldn't have been surprised when I found a woman sat behind the receptionist's desk doing what I found her doing.

Her eyes glared blankly through dark-red hair toward a static computer screen. She didn't respond as I approached and asked her quietly, desperately for help. She was simply sat there, pale-white, absently staring, both her hands toying with her naked breasts. She was playing with and picking apart, dissecting with long, fake fingernails, the flesh of her swollen and erect nipples. I should at this point have left. I knew all of what I would see. But I *had* to go further, I had to and I don't know why.

Further into the hospital, where television screens were mounted high on waiting room walls, I found a large crowd of people, and all around, I noticed, in the illuminated dark corners scattered distantly about, the bustling figures in distant, ill-lit darkness to be shapes of people, the shared sources of that cacophony of strange grunts and quiet cries I could hear everywhere bounding off the walls.

Patients, doctors, nurses and cleaners all stood or sat gathered staring up at the screens high on the walls of the waiting room I had come upon. One man, nearest to me when I found him with my eyes, was laying on the floor with his head raised to watch the screens of static up high—both his legs broken. The crowd I could fully see before me were naught but a swarm of faces, pale and consumed, contorted in emotion, desire, fixation contoured with the starkly horrifying masochistic pleasure and numbness of mind I had seen previously in the anxious smile of my father as he too had stared at a blank television screen of static blacks and greys. *Lunacy!* Confusion, disorientation; madly driven and stuck to the spot they each occupied, and yet all seemingly vacant eyed, all masturbating, tantalising oneself or another.

I don't care much to share the details of horrors I saw within that hospital as I staggered about searching for an exit, *without my flashlight!* for I had dropped it somewhere in the dark of my panic near that crowd in the waiting room. I can't remember all of what I actually saw them doing. No no I don't want to and I won't try. How it feels to me a haze of sickness I once glanced at in a nightmare, half there in my mind in every waking moment I have existed in since.

For the love of God…. How could people tear into themselves LIKE THIS, O' HUMANITY; and in such a manner so depriving and wretched—WHAT *CURSED TOXINS* WERE IN THAT RAIN?!

I left the building swiftly, laughing aloud and grave. I felt, I felt as though I'd never awoken earlier in my conservatory, like I'd died under the spell of that red rain, I felt...

as though I, Ryan Elliott-Walker, would *never* again soundly sleep or wake, that it would be no longer possible; and in one word I named this madness I was finding within myself:

'Theneverendingcirclingpain.'

Like I said, I left the building, quickly, laughing gravely, loudly at all I had seen... and, fortunately, I had been too horrified as to what I might find to go the rest of the journey to my mother's house, and so... I did not go; I did not witness my mother and eldest brother mindlessly engaged in unspeakable behaviours.... I did not go.

I didn't think much after I left the hospital carpark, to be wholly honest. I just drove home, and when I got there, I parked the car in the drive and left my dad, without even checking on him, or remembering his being there on the back seat at all, unconscious and still wrapped in his blood-soaked quilt.

I went into the house, through the front door; locked it. I headed upstairs to my bedroom where I latched the door and ignored all night the long-drawn howls rising through the floor.

The moment my head touched the pillow, I fell asleep.

FEBRUARY 24TH, THE KNOCKING AT THE DOOR

The following morning I awoke to a red mist inside my bedroom. The Rain had seemingly poured whilst I'd slept, and my window, I saw, with alarm, that I had left it open. My bedroom door *too!* was unlatched when I looked, closed but not locked as I had first left it before passing out late in the night.

I remember awakening throughout that first night to a constant pelleting of rain at my windowsill, and loud crashes and bangs coming from the front door, but I was delirious from the day's crazed turnings and could only but simmer to the surface of the night before I fell back again beneath the safety of closed eyelids and dreamless sleep.

It hadn't been The Rain causing those loud crashes and bangs, I now realised. Someone, with their fists, was knocking at the front door.

"Who is it?" I called with a dry croak of my voice as I hurriedly made my way down the staircase.

"You left me outside all night!" I heard from the other side. "Open the door, please. I'm feeling better... I'm sorry you saw what you saw, Ryan...."

I shouldn't have opened the door for my father, but he had sounded so convincingly frail and hapless and sorry.... He had sounded sane!

And then, just before I opened the door, after turning the lock, I heard him say, quietly, and to himself, like he could not help it—as though we were back in the living room again, he masturbating under the glare of the living room light, and I perplexed:

"Turn it off, turn it off."

The quiet mutter of his voice assailed me with a horrible feeling, but it was too late to close and lock the door again; for before the door was even open enough for me to see faintly a fraction of the sky, I saw first the red drops dripping from the bridge of my father's pale-white nose, and his unkindly smile beaming brightly into the house as he dropped the quilt he'd been using to hide his nakedness. He lurched at me through the gap, flinging the door wide and forcing me onto the staircase behind.

At first I didn't know whether he meant to attack me or simply gain way back into the house. He stood over me, sniffing the air like an animal. He looked about frantically, his shoulders were raised to his ears, forearms outstretched at right angles, fingers flexing. And then his eyes snapped onto me laying on my back against the staircase and he opened his mouth wide to snarl my name. He clicked his jaw open and shut; blood spat onto me as he sliced and clipped his own tongue between the clacking of his teeth: "RYAN ELLIOTT-WALKER," he bellowed as he rained blood onto my face, "YOU ARE NOT INFECTED." His voice was an ominous, deep tone from within his chest; my father, like a possessed speaker phone, did not seem to be speaking from or of himself.

I tried to crawl backward and stand but he was too close over me, reaching for me with his pallid hands. And again he spoke my name, "RYAN ELLIOTT-WALKER!" in three guttural croaks, before lurching suddenly forward to come crashing down atop of me, his arms and fingers horribly tensed. I caught him in the grips of my hands and held him above me, his jaw continuing to clack. His tongue no longer there between his teeth, for being half serrated, a thick steam of blood ran down his chin to spill across my face and neck.

"Ryan Elliott-Walker Ryan Elliott-WALKER, you are not infected." Eyes wide, pupils dilated, his head suddenly jerked forward, his lips pulled back, teeth gnawing desperately for my neck. I pulled my legs into my chest and kicked upward, hurtling him into the air. He hit the front door frame and fell to the side. I scrambled to my feet and shot up the staircase.

Retreating to my bedroom, I then relocked my door and closed my window swiftly.

The mist had evaporated but its scent was still within my room. It had been outside also, the smell, from behind my father before he pushed open the door, and upon his breath when he set upon me on the stairs, I just didn't taste it, smell it as strongly until I was back in my bedroom. Stood in the silence of my room I could but smell the scent like I never had before; the smell, like rotten limbs of air, crippled me with a sickening feeling I have so far begun to portray in these pages,—the sickness that ripens in my gut.

I covered my nose with my t-shirt to lessen the smell, and though it helped, it did not completely silence the reek. The next moment, my father could be heard limping, taking docile, heavy steps hurriedly upstairs— well, he wasn't as my 'father' anymore, was he? He was... something else, something rabid, filled with frenzy, 'possessed' is the best way to put it. And before I'd managed to gain a grip of myself, to fully rid my lungs of that crippling smell, of all the dizziness and sickness with it that had overcome me, he was standing outside my door: "*Knock knock knock,*" he *grumbled* in deep, quick tones from outside my room.

Then he began to actually knock; KNOCK KNOCK, KNOCK KNOCK, KNOCK KNOCK, at my door, and the noise filled my ears like I was centre to some mad drum! The air of my room pulsed strangely, particles of red bursting into sight and then, again, there were none, nothing but the smell of The Rain within my room. He stopped knocking after several horrific minutes.

"Oh El, we know you can hear us. Open up the door so we can have a little talk, Ryan-El. We promise we only want to speak… there's something strange you're going to find quite funny, actually! my son."
Feral. Deranged. He was not my father when he said these words. I remember this point with such clarity. The sound of his voice as he formed each word—as though someone was pushing and pulling every syllable out of his throat, each word covered in sounds of phlegm and spattered blood. The room was spinning about me still. The smell, that vile, putrid odour still in my lungs! I backed from the door and hung out of my window, gasping for clean air, gripping the window frame tight as not to fall as my head spun and spun and I felt that sickness, whatever it is, strange and curdling in my stomach, extenuating down to my feet and up to my head.

What was I to do? Kill him, my father? if I can call him that! He still wore the same flesh, the same face, of course. And what if he tore into me with his teeth, as he had tried to gnaw on my neck once before, then what… well, I have refrained from the disease so far, I thought, and I can't continue without taking a chance, a risk, every second out of my bedroom may be a risk! And so, I opened the cupboard where I stored, beneath a pile of clothes and in a chest, things that I would need out there to survive—like I've told you, I had been paranoid of something like this, an apocalypse of sorts, for years.

I pulled out 4ft of rope, wrapped the ends around my shaking hands to form a bridge I could use to restrain him.

The next job was unlatching the door.

I did it loud and fast, stepped two paces back and waited. Whatever it was in his brain producing those words, well, I figured he or they would have more use of hisself than would be believable of a simply deranged, deluded, suffering wreck as had been his previous state and all those people I witnessed endlessly toying with themselves or one another in that hospital! But he didn't touch the handle, did not anything but bray on the blasted door, I tell you!

I waited a number of minutes to see whether this was or was not a trick, to see if he was simply biding his time, trying to cleverly elude me, and take my mind by surprise when he quickly opens and dives through the door. But he didn't do a thing other than bray, obsessively, like it was his last order before the turning off of cogs and signals in his brain; returning to the obsessive creature I had witnessed jerking to the static glow of our television a previous day past.

I didn't open the door myself. I was smarter than to face him head on, as I did not know to what extent he may charge at me, to what capacity he would see me as a threat or a meal of sorts to chew! His ferocity, as with any feral and unknown creature, was to be treat with utmost caution.

I climbed out of my window instead (noting to my self that the smell of The Rain was no longer present within my bedroom, and feeling in myself somewhat, remarkably, better). My head had cleared, sickness no longer beseeched and riddled me swaying and dizzy. I climbed onto the porch over our front door and carefully lowered myself down and then let go, dropping to the ground, carefully and quietly. I then opened the front door, walked back into the house, up the stairs, constantly listening to my father's loud knocks upon my bedroom door, for a change in them, but he gave no sign of recognition as to my approach.

It was easy enough, really. I quietly approached him from behind, raised the rope over his delirious, enraged figure as he proceeded to hammer my steadily cracking door with his left fist, and brought it down over his front and around his arms. Next, I dragged him carefully but securely, as not to injure him, down the stairs and into the kitchen where I tied him with the rope to one of the dinning table chairs.

His face stared at me, unseeing of who I was; *his son*. He was not there, his expression twisted, unchanging. So I shouted. I lost it, momentarily. My father, a pale, enraged, feral creature. Perhaps he was dazed, I thought. I had just interrupted his knocking with a rather quick and probably dizzying drag down a flight of stairs.

"Who are you!" I blared. "Say your name. Say your name. *Say it*." His eyes became fixed on me. Still, however, he remained unresponsive. Then he began to sniff the air. "Say it say your—" I became breathless and had to pause, my voice too loud, blood surging too keenly to my head. I felt, in the next moment, rather horribly dizzy. I faced away, lent on the kitchen worktop over our fridge, and when I faced back, his mouth was trying to move.

"Say your name," I said again. "Who are you!"

"Not dead," he replied, his voice a quiet mutter.

"Who are you," I said again, quieter this time.

"Not dead." A laugh, quiet, maybe a gurgle of blood deep in his throat? I don't know, but it came with the same words, and it sounded much like a quiet laugh.

"Say your name say Andr—"

"You are not infected. They'll come for you, El. They'll be coming soon enough." Who is they? I thought, the room making me feel sick as I stared into my father's dim blue, bloodshot eyes.

"Who!?" I shouted.

He laughed, and this time it was most definitely a laugh. Blood filled to his mouth, and his lips peeled back to show his teeth. He became viscous in his seat, struggling, eyes brightening.

The chair rocked and rocked, threatening to tip over. I manoeuvred myself around him carefully and grabbed the chair from behind as he tried to lean and turn toward me to tear at my skin with the want of flexing jaws.

I pushed the chair from kitchen to living room, quickly; turned on the television, and he became quiet, even as I readjusted and repositioned his seat at an appreciative distance from the glare of the television screen he remained so;—only when did I turn the light on did he turn to show me signs of violence and discomfort, turning his head sharply and with mouth baring a wide and snarling yawn—but I flicked the light back off quickly and never heard any sort of guttural or hissing sound pass those pale, pale lips.

THE MYSTERIOUS NOTES

After the morning I'd had with my father, I didn't feel all that hungry for breakfast and, checking the oven clock, I saw it was nearing 11 A. M. anyhow. Yesterday had certainly taken its toll on me. I don't know what time it was I arrived home, or even the time it had been when I awoke in the conservatory before rushing my father to the hospital. I had hopefully slept for several hours, despite my father's loud knocking on the front door!

Outside, through the kitchen window, the sky that morning looked clear (which was actually more worrying to me—as normal rain came from clouds it seemed, and this other stuff, red and toxic, *The Rain*, did not). The sunshine looked welcoming and so did the clear air free from the discolouring of a red mist.

Rocky! I remember thinking with a hurried feeling, as I recalled her barking greeting me as I had arrived home late the previous night, and how I had completely ignored her. I opened the conservatory door and there she was, asleep. "Rocky, Rocky," I whispered. Her ears moved and eyes opened. "I'm sorry girl, I almost forgot about you in here," I said as I sat down next to her on the conservatory couch. She yawned wide and sat up next to me, turning to stare blankly at me. "Thirsty?" I asked.

I filled her bowl at the sink and opened the door of the conservatory and headed into the back garden where I placed her water on the ground for her and breathed in the fresh air to quench my own thirst. Fresh and clean was the air. Silent and waiting were the streets and the surrounding gardens about my home. No noise, no cars, no sound anywhere could I hear. And then I was taken by surprise; a flock of birds swooped low in their flight, tweeting shrill, tweeting sharp in the arc of their descent, the garden next door to mine.

Curious, I thought. Curious, for I nor anybody else had seen birds or critters of any kind in urban parts for sometime, and with the catastrophe that came, which they had tried to avoid (or avoid *us*, might I suggest), there I had just seen, healthy and together, a flock of birds owning the only sound and flexing there wings in the air all theirs.

I opened the back gate and ventured onto the drive. The doors of my father's car were shut but for the rear driver's side. I had drove straight onto the drive last night, parking somewhat askew! and had forgotten to shut the garden gate. My father's quilt lay around the corner of the house, on the path between the front door and the front gate, stained dark-red.

I rolled up the quilt to put in the outside bin, but before that I walked to the tree, tall and old, sitting centre of our side garden, overlooking fields and roads. I lent upon its trunk familiar to me. I looked up at the clear blue sky and around the landscape (our home was atop a gradual, high slope); it was a sight like you could never have witnessed before; daylight and no sound, no movement but for the wind and the grass and leaves on trees, bushes, no movement but green movement, concrete buildings, roads, in the distance and close, all the air, completely silent… like the eye of a storm was passing overhead, but that was just because of the televisions. Without the static drawing people like bugs, the world would have surely been a different picture. Again, that question, I have asked myself countlessly, I found perspiring in my mind: Where did The Rain come from?

I happened upon a note then, nailed to the tree, and with crisp and clear handwriting it read:

'Angels never came
no wings shaded men
nothing but The Rain
torrent of blood from the sky
a toxic spew of waste
death and madness!
our shame.'

The note was singed, 'Lu Tien Oloiv'. Who? I thought, ripping the note from the trunk of the tree. And then the paper looked familiar, and I turned it around to find on the back an old shopping list written by my father. Someone was in my house? I thought. My bedroom door was unlatched! Window slightly open when I awoke… could they have climbed in when I slept?

I put the note in my pocket, scared from that point on that someone might be watching and following me. I looked to the supermarket down the hill and across a field; Asda, situated at the end of a long stretch of road, perpendicular to an old Catholic church. I noted then the next of peculiarities to come on the day of February 24th:

30

a pyramid trailing high a black spiral of smoke, outside the front entrance to the supermarket.

The thought of driving there with Rocky had been at the forefront of my unspoken mind since I had awoken. But this shape, burning pile, I could see. What is it? I thought, who has formed it? The same that left me this note?

My questions were answered later,—but only with the need for more answers to questions that still linger over and shadow me as I here and now write these words. Nothing has become certain quickly.

#

Before heading back indoors, I retrieved my clothes I yesterday in panic had thrown away, and found that they were not stained and nor did they any longer smell. My father's quilt, however, I had to throw away, as it was so awfully stained with his blood. After then showering thoroughly dried blood from my neck and hands, putting my now salvaged clothes in the washing machine, changing into an aged pair of denim jeans I found at the bottom of my wardrobe, a pair of brown boots, a white t-shirt and my father's old, brown leather jacket he'd had since his days in the R. A. F., I found myself following the road that ran along the side of the Catholic church I have previously, once mentioned. I Rolled to a dead stop in my father's navy blue Rover 45. as the tarmac came to an end, the main entrance of the supermarket coming into clear view through a gap of bushes and trees from across a breadth of pavement and road. I thought it best to take a closer look, you see, before pursuing blindly into the unknown of the carpark.

Rocky had stared at me the whole drive down the road. It wasn't just a simple stare though. Her *eyes*, how they seemed to *see* me, as though assessing me....

I got out of the car and opened the boot. From a grey rucksack I had packed I took out a pair of binoculars and walked up to the path before the road ahead. I crouched before the bushes and began to scan the supermarket and carpark for movement. The carpark was full of parked, abandoned cars but no persons. And then, I could see the pyramid and all of its twisted shapes, like limbs and charred faces, black and smouldering; dead things, maybe animals, I thought, maybe not....

Before I could consider anything more about what I had seen, a noise alerted me from behind and I spun around to see Rocky's car door flinging open. She leapt out from the passenger seat and paced around the car. She stopped outside the closed and silent gates of the church graveyard. She looked over to me, her eyes tense, alert as they met my own.

I dashed toward her. She was glaring into the graveyard. She barked loudly at something I could not see, her chestnut fur a bright fire-orange in the sun, her small and stocky Staffordshire-Terrier build perfectly still. Before I had reached the gates, the sound of a door heavily crashing open and a man's panicked voice rushed over the walls of the graveyard. Rocky jumped up at the graveyard gates, barking louder, pawing the iron bars.

"Help, help!" cried the man's voice. I opened one side of the gates and stepped into the graveyard, Rocky remaining by my side and growling. The vicar of the church came dashing toward me. "Help, help," he called without seeing me. And then a second man, clad in a torn white t-shirt and gardener gloves, his lower half bare and crusted with dry blood, came slouched and quickly limping from out the church's dark doorway.

The priest stumbled. He ran into the side of a gravestone. His eyes finally caught mine. "Please," he called out, and then the man pursuing him was upon him, and, like a crazed dog, sunk teeth into the vicar's upper left arm. I ran forward, leapt over a gravestone and ran into the half-naked gardener, knocking him from atop the wailing priest. "Thank God, thank God," murmured the priest as I put myself before him and he crawled behind me exclaiming in pain.

I pulled a hunting knife from the sheath about my waist. The crazed gardener started to get up, but, before he could gain his feet, Rocky sank her jaws into his neck and began shaking him like an unpleasant chew toy. The gardener moaned and clawed for Rocky, tried to grab her with gloved hands, but his neck soon broke and Rocky let him go. The gardener didn't move an inch other than to twitch as his crooked neck gushed with blood into the soil, and I was sure he was dead.

I turned around to help the priest up, when he quietly trembled, "Behind, more, more." I turned to see two dark figures come screaming into daylight from out the darkness of the church. Two women, identical in their horror, long blonde heads of hair to which both locks and chunks of scalpel were missing. Eyes squinting half-shut for the outdoor brightness. Their faces were wretched, pale, drawn. They looked about; and unable to see, they began to sniff the air.

"They haven't seen us," I said to the priest, "stay low." I put my hand on Rocky's back and made her sit. "Stay," I whispered to her. And then I began, on crouched legs, to make my way past gravestones as these two deranged, grotesque spectres of women lurched across the graveyard. With hunting knife in hand I slowly stood up before one of them, a gravestone between us, and then her eyes, squinting in the bright daylight, managed to see me! For the next moment she was hissing and spitting flecks of blood on my face, her eyes opening dreadfully wide.

Her mouth flared open and I brought my hunting knife across into her left temple, pulled it out and turned to my right. The second woman looked around and glared at me, her eyes wide and bloodshot. She burst forward, screeching shrill and sharp, hands reaching out like the talons of some viscous bird. She knocked me backwards, grabbing my face with one hand, my right shoulder with her other. I knocked her right arm away with my left, and taking her prying hand from my face, finger nails scratching me horribly in the process. Quickly, I grabbed her neck with my left hand, whereby I held her at a distance, and I thrust my knife deep into her chest.

She smiled at me. She smiled! Her eyes were wide open, dull and horrible, bloodshot and staring into my own. Her lips curled and teeth gleamed red. I thought for a second that I could feel the final palpitations of her heart shimmer down the blade and through the handle of my knife, and then strangely through my own flesh and bones, like a static shock or ripple.

She went limp in my hold and I let go of my grip and just let her fall to the floor like a broken doll, and I was sure she was dead.

"Praise God, praise God!" I heard from behind. "The Heavenly Father sent you, you of people, to do his bidding, his saving, reaping, praise the Lord! I turned to face him, the priest, and watched with blood trickling across my left eye as he scurried along the dirt upon his knees to the rabid gardener my dog had left bleeding in the soil. "My child, rest, rest," said the priest as he tried to close the dead man's eyes, but they wouldn't shut and simply kept opening to a dull and bloodshot glare, "rest now, rest. The Father knows all truth, he knows of you, of me, he holds the light and what is to come." He stopped trying to close the dead man's eyes upon the ground and instead turned to lightly cover his face, eyes and open mouth with a handful of dirt.

"Bless you, sir, bless you!" he said, rising to his feet, struggling toward me.

"You're welcome," I replied.

"Bless you and your presence but know, too, you have sinned, know we have all, even I, and yet the two of us, WE, we stand unaffected by this disease this… *curse*…. Like the rapture we are somehow its vessels, sir. I dreamt of you and of this, last night before the blood rain began for the second time. Bless you sir, bless you."

"You dreamt of this?" I asked.

The vicar bent down, collected two handfuls of dirt and gently poured them over the two dead faces of the women. "Tut, tut, tut," he clicked with his tongue as he covered with dirt from his hands the still open eyes and wide snarling mouths of the women I had slain. "Yes, yes I did, I dreamt of you, that dog, too, blood other than the rains.... That's how I knew to come here, you see, I was waiting for you—doing what I must."

"That's interesting... queer... but, honestly? Can you believe what you're saying to me? You... you *dreamt* of this. And what about your arm, did you dream of that too? You look a little pale, are you okay?"

"My arm troubles me not."

"Anything or *anyone* left inside the church?"

"Nothing but a dead woman I found these people here... doing things to.... Defiling, and... you really don't want to see, my child, it isn't pretty."

"Okay. Well, I was just investigating the carpark before heading over, into the supermarket." I wiggled the binoculars that were slung around my neck. "If you want, you can come with me.... Or I can take you somewhere—"

"No problem, no problem. And yes. I am to come with you until I know more, I believe.... I must grab my bag however. I left it inside by the altar," said the priest, and he walked into the church.

I put my knife back into the sheath about my waist and looked around at the three bodies. The gardener, with a large chunk missing from the neck, lay awkwardly several meters from the women. All had open eyes, now covered in dirt. All had open, gaping mouths, covered, lightly filled with dirt. Each looked stiff where they lay, frozen, as though death had filled their limbs like cement—or, it was as though they lied in wait, for The Rain to come and quicken them.

I left the graveyard through the gate I had come. Rocky followed me to the car. She climbed in at the passenger side, and I closed the door. I went back to the pavement before the bushes where I had first stood with binoculars in hand, and gave the carpark and supermarket entrance another sweeping check. Clear, I noted, nothing in sight, no deranged, no persons, not even the pyramid that had so intrigued me was any longer burning from within; for the smoke of it was now white.

I put the binoculars back in my rucksack and closed the boot of the car. The priest was still inside the church and I decided, after waiting a few minutes, to go inside and see what the delay was about.

As soon as I walked in through the open back door to the church, I heard a voice bouncing loudly around the hollow building and off the walls. "Revelation 12:9," I heard. "And the great dragon was cast out!" I walked into the light beaming down through colourful stained windows and saw the priest stood at the altar. "That old serpent, called the Devil, and Satan, which deceiveth the whole world," he blared at empty pews. "He was hurled to the earth, and his angels with him. Revelation 20:1, And I saw an angel come down from heaven, having the key of the bottomless pit and a great chain in his hand! Revelation 1:7, *behold!*"—I noticed a woman lying in the aisle; I approached her, ignoring the priest as he continued—"he cometh with clouds; and every eye shall see him, and they also which pierced him: and all kindreds of the earth shall wail because of him. Even so, Amen." I crouched by the woman whom was half-hidden in the darkness of the floor. "Amen!" the priest's voice echoed. I turned her over, and she was dead. Her eyes met mine when I lifted her head up and from out the shadows, and they were filled with pain and rage, her body felt stiff like a plank, and her chest was gaping where her heart should have been. I dropped her heavy corpse back to the church floor when I noticed this and the full smell of death reeking from the wound. And then I saw, sticking out her mouth, a crumpled piece of paper.

I pulled the paper out with two fingers, uncreased it on one knee and was just about to try and read the words in a dim beam of light, before the priest assailed me from behind, screaming, "Get off her! Get off her, you creature. Leave her blood alone." He was hitting me with a bible and screaming in my ears. I turned around, covering my head, and shouted 'stop' at him, twice! But he kept on wailing and then began to cry. "Leave her, leave her," he wailed and spat. "She's not for you, she wasn't meant to be dead." He backed away from me, carrying in his right hand a large duffle bag, and turned and ran for the back door of the church.

"Stop," I shouted, stationary in the hollowness of the church, amidst the echo of footsteps, but he was out of sight fast, and I had to chase him.

"No, no please," he cried as he ran, craning his neck to see me, "help! Someone!" He made it as far as the graveyard gate after stumbling into three gravestones and falling helplessly into the graveyard wall. "Please please please," he cried, trying to scramble to his feet.

"I'm not going to hurt you," I said. "Who was that woman inside?"

"My—my—," he whimpered, struggling to continue. "I watched it drain her, they—they chased me when I tried to stop them. But she was already dead, I found her like that and then they were there. Someone killed her and kept her heart. I couldn't find it I couldn't find it."

"There's no need to be scared now," I said, "please, come get in my car, I can take you to my house where you'll be safe. Okay?"

"Okay... okay," said the priest, looking up through pale-blue eyes, his face spattered with blood and hands notably more. I noticed, too, his clerical collar no longer a white square but a crimson stain. He walked to my car like a man convicted of heinous crimes. He was quiet as we drove up the hill to my father's home. Just before I got out the car and after coming to a stop in the drive, I took the note I had found in the dead woman's mouth from my jean pocket, and quietly read to myself:

'Fear the black heart's beat,
know to dread The Rain.'

Again, the note was signed: Lu Tien Oloiv.

#

I brought the priest in through the front door and upstairs to the spare bedroom. He needed to sleep he had said as we came inside. I left him in my brother's old bedroom (now the 'guest room', since he departed last

September for university) and closed the door. The priest hadn't said anything else to me other than that he needed to sleep. I had, however, told him to stay in my brother's bedroom until I returned, and that I wouldn't be long.

I didn't want him venturing downstairs to find my father bound to a chair before the static glow of our television screen. But he had looked extremely weary (I couldn't help but feel it was part from his wound, too, his *demeanour*; the assault upon me, the running, begging, and now the extreme fatigue), so, I left him to sleep and I set back down the road to the supermarket, as I had first intended to.

I didn't bother with another reconnaissance mission. Instead, I quietly rolled into the car park, keeping a lookout as I did. The carpark was at least half-full. Silence, like everywhere else, was the only thing to greet me.

I parked close to the trolley bay and got out of the car, my feet sounding loud beneath me as they touched down on the concrete. Rocky opened her door and I heard her leap out from the passenger's side. I went to the boot and opened it, taking from out its contents my katana I had decided to take along after the encounter at the church. A longer blade meant I didn't have to get so up-close-and-personal to fend off the deranged.

I slung the katana over my back and walked the corner of the trolley bay. There it was at the other end of the trolley bay, before the entrance to the supermarket. I saw the limbs, black and twisted, faces peering from within; dead. I saw it to be naught other than a pyramid of dead bodies piled one atop another. And *someone* had set them alight, *someone* had piled them.

I walked around the mound, covering my nose with my t-shirt; the smell was putrid, singed flesh; vile and rotten, the odour of The Rain, hiding somewhere in the pile of collected bodies, too. Faces were hard to make out, arms and legs only recognisable from one another by the digits—curled fingers for arms, blackened toes for legs. Crisp and black and charred and trailing high a dying ladder of white smoke.

I got away from it fast, running, half stumbling as I went, toward the supermarket entrance, terrified to my gut. I almost chucked up, coughing loudly, my throat filling with sick like it had the time The Rain first fell and I tumbled sliding onto the ground puking my guts up, that vile stench filling my nostrils like it had.

The supermarket doors opened as I approached them, and I looked up to see bloody streaks all leading out the entrance, across the supermarket floor, like a hundred bodies had been butchered and dragged outside, one by one. It was clear where all the bodies had come from in that one moment—that someone had been and done me a favour, someone had cleared out the supermarket of all the infected. (Though a favour as I recount, not for a moment could I find it favourable all to which I saw; only that in was I spared the viscous attack of any more a deranged countenance, feral fellow upon the earth, my visit to the supermarket, as had I seen from mine father and the parishioner.)

I'd been hoping, since my trip to the hospital, that I'd just be able to walk past them all, wherever I encountered them; so long as they were preoccupied with a television, I knew this to be hopeful; that, for as long as the power did stay on, the deranged would remain docile and content within the static glow I was seeing everywhere, just as I could see now the screens up high on walls of the supermarket blaring down their static greys and whites that perplexed the infected and deranged so. But after the encounter I'd had at the church, after my father attacking me that very morning, I was growing more and more doubtful as to the lack of hostility I'd been hoping for. And whoever had done this here, I thought, murdered and burnt all of those people and piled them high, a small, black and charred human pyramid, had either taken advantage of the infected's docile state, or defended theirselves like I had from my own father and three times further in the graveyard of the Catholic church. But why had they burnt them?... And then I found another note.

Beneath a stack of red metal cans of gasoline, six in total, one empty, five full, a piece of paper I pulled out from beneath one, and I read out loud, (the same handwriting I had found twice already that day):

'That which is charred
has no muscles at all'

Who is this guy and what is he talking about? I thought, my grip threatening to tear the note apart in anger. *Lu Tien Oloiv Lu Tien Oloiv*, who does that name belong to?! '*That which is charred has no muscles at all*'—I tore up the note and threw it aside. Before I entered the supermarket with Rocky I scanned the carpark behind me for any sign of movement, a follower, anyone watching me from afar. But there was nobody there and I quickly walked further inside.

I found myself a shopping trolley, abandoned, close to the entrance, empty. There wasn't anything too strangely amiss inside. Other than large patches and spots of blood grouped together here and there, nothing had been looted, nothing smashed and broken (there was some disorder... trolleys half-full, empty, brimming, left in all kinds of places, cans of food and other such things fallen to the floor, here and there), but other than all that, the supermarket just felt untidy, unkept, unmanned.

I picked out a large bag of dry dog food for Rocky, a couple of crates of bottled spring water, plenty of bananas, as many nutritional protein bars as I could, six frozen steaks, and two fresh salmon and tuna steaks. I wasn't in a hurry to loot the entire store. I only took what I did need.

Going through the checkouts and bagging all my supplies in the eerie silence that seemed to drift, glide over me, through the vacant isles and the vacant checkouts, was one of the most unusual feelings I've ever had. I took my wallet out of my back pocket and just threw it on the cashier's empty chair. Didn't think I'd be needing it anymore... maybe I was trying to shed off the odd feeling I'd gained from looting, I don't know, but either way, it had made me feel easier as I walked out of the supermarket with my trolley of looted goods; loudly squeaking wheels and rattling metal frame of my trolley the only noise as I passed the silent and charred pyramid of the dead.

BLACK HEART BEAT

It was late in the afternoon when I heard the priest stir. I'd been sitting on the top stair to the landing. Tired and depleted, yet I didn't feel hungry, hadn't eaten, had only drank a bottle of the water I looted, and yet I didn't or hadn't felt thirsty. I didn't know what I felt, other than dread and darkness, surrealism, a dream, and yet… complete wakefulness.

I stood up, stretched, yawned, looked out the window at the top of the stairs. Sunset was nearing, the sky held a purple tinge across the horizon and light was growing dimmer. I went downstairs. Figured the priest would come wandering down, looking for me. I'd already jammed the living room handle from the other side with a broom so that he couldn't just walk in and find my father sat alone in the dark. I left a note stuck to the door, too, saying, 'Go round back'.

I opened the front door and left it wide for the priest. The front gates were shut. The house was in order. Meat stocked the freezer, fish and eggs the fridge, bananas and oranges and grapes, strawberries, and two sticky-toffee puddings the cupboards and water the pantry. Rocky hadn't eaten either….

I felt so weary as I walked outdoors, exhausted. *Numb* would be a good word to throw in here. I wasn't hungry, thirsty, in fact, my stomach felt sick, painful even, as if brewing with all the catastrophe and vile happenings and stench of the past few days. I didn't feel anything much further than that, any kind of distraught feeling for my father, any worry for my mother, for my two brothers. I felt wretched and weak and sick, unsure of my safety for all that *surrounded* me, for the unknown dread in a world suddenly turned holocaust; The Rain; the infected; the people-less streets; the fucking notes!— all the things I couldn't yet explain. I had hope my mother and brothers were still alive.

If someone had been in my house, too, last night, climbing through my window and unlatched my bedroom door, then how safe was I in my own home, or anywhere—if I am being followed? Maybe, maybe I'd been sleep walking, I thought, looking up to the clear, dark blue sky, beginning to feel calmer and sleepier with the coming lateness of the evening. *Maybe my stalker is benevolent.*

I walked over to the tree sitting centre of the side garden, and, with a wave of amusement, and then horror, I noticed what my stalker had left for me before I had the chance to take in the sunset just cresting the far and purple horizon. A black heart dangled from a low branch by a blood soaked string. It was black as night, dark as coal; dark like the sodden and untrod mud of a marsh. I stopped perfectly still to inspect it as it swung gently back and forth in the breeze. The exterior of the flesh was covered with blue and faint lines, *electric-blue*. I felt... blissful staring at it, the hypnotic colours, such strange allure. And then it beat, inches from my face. It just contracted, just like that, *bu-dum*, once, hard. I stepped back, watching closely as the blue veins became bluer, brightening, and it beat again, and then again, faster, then faster, until it rocked back and forth frantically on the string, not to the wind, but to its own perpetual beating.

I was staring with wide eyes when I remembered the note I'd found in the dead woman's mouth. 'Fear the black heart beat, know to dread The Rain.' I backed away and looked up at the sky, and before it hit my face, I saw it coming. I saw a purple sky consumed by red, the earth in shadow. I stumbled off the grass, slipping in the slickness of The Rain as it drenched all things red and shattered the stillness of twilight with a crashing monotony.

A figure through the red falling haze came toward me as I made for the front door. The priest had awoken. He hurled his body at me weakly, convulsing and shivering madly. And he screamed, he screamed over and over, "It's coming, it's coming, it's coming," over and over. I tried to drag him inside but he started flailing as I did, The Rain disguising everything around me red and making it all the more harder to move and navigate. I tried to restrain him and pull him indoors but it was no use as he flung his arms about madly toward the sky, slipping and sliding in the cascading wetness, hurling himself all around. I had to hit him around the head twice before he went limp.

I dragged his unconscious body back inside and watched from the front door as The Rain poured and poured, and then that rotting, putrid smell began to erupt in my nostrils and fill my doorway with its stench. As I closed the door against the pressing weight of rain, darkness drifting like a slow shroud over all the earth, I swore I heard a screech cry my name from out the columns of falling rain high in the sky somewhere distant, somewhere far.

FEBRUARY 25TH

I awoke from an eye, searching and magnificent, high above the ground, over the streets that I had lived. I awoke in terror and sweat, like a hospital patient full of sickness and weary; and again, as a new day had awoke me from slumber, I did not feel my hunger stir nor my thirst yearn—but the sickness in my gut.

I got from my bed stretching, yawned and felt myself fully awakened, fully rejuvenated. Outside there was no red mist. The air was clean, clear. In my house all, too, seemed settled and fine, nothing amiss, my door latched, windows closed; no inside mist. The priest hadn't awoken at this time, it was just I. And since I had dragged his weak and flailing self back inside, knocking him first unconscious, and laid him to sleep, I was suspicious that he might lay asleep for sometime for the heat, and delirium, that he had surely radiated. My dog, too, was slumbering deeply, it seemed, laid at the top of the staircase, fidgeting and unsettled in whatever dreams had taken her.

How I had similarly passed out last night as to the like of the night before when I returned home from the hospital. The Rain fell, and how my spirit had felt so drained, how I had not eaten, and how now I was awake, energised, as if by some mistake, as though my body was being fed—but by what? Dreams? Dreams of a great and soaring eye like I had witnessed in slumber for the first time throughout the night of February 24th; a dream where I had occupied the skies and gazed with watching eye, soaring, sailing and gazing through columns of red pouring rain; a vision, a dream, an entity alive. For all that time I had felt a threat beneath as I gazed, my sight searching rapidly…. Dreams, I thought, only a fool would follow dreams and think them *real*, not I. And like that I shook away the seamless dream-like delusion of that watching eye, a shiver running down my spine as I did so, and made downstairs for the kitchen to break fast.

In panic, I realised, I had not locked the front door last night. A danger, now that I knew or suspected that someone might be following myself. The heart was still on the string when I passed through the drive to avoid my father within the living room. I approached the tree and removed it and took it inside with me. I knew what it was; an infected heart, probably belonging to the gaping hole in the chest of the dead woman I found within the church. I was finally beginning to grow a suspicion that this man following me, Lu, could only be a friend; but there was another presence I felt, one with enmity.

Fear the black heart beat, know to dread The Rain.

So, now I had a means of forecasting, be it only moments before, The Rain. And how hideous it is to get caught in that slime of red downpour, and its putrid smell like some toxic spew, which filled your gut. I thought not much more on the advantages of what I had gained through the note and the infected heart, thought not of what The Rain could do to the living caught in its wake outdoors, or do to the infected themselves; for I was still to discover two things.

I did not know how the heart would last, if it would rot and shrivel and reek, or, if like it's black flesh suggested, its infected like, that it would somehow last—kept black and alien, electric-blue lines faintly covering the specimen; an undead, demonic possession of flesh. I wrapped it in cling film and placed it on a plate in the fridge. I had plans later to make of its diced flesh necklaces, so that it could be better carried with ease, and about the neck, an electric-blue, pulsating warning, a contracting glowing of flesh to tell of The Rain, to swing at my neck. But first, I had breakfast to make, and I didn't much fancy putting myself off eating when I had no hunger for it already—so the heart remained in the fridge, upon a plate, wrapt in cling film.

#

An hour later, I had eaten breakfast; eggs, toast, a sliced banana and honey. I drank a litre of water. I could feel the contents of my stomach heavy and indigestible, the water swishing sickly inside of me as I walked back outside, around the house, through the front door and then up the stairs to check on my dog and the priest. My whole body, like the pain I've documented already, like when I was in the hospital and all I saw made me feel so sick, that *sickness* brewing each day in my stomach. I decided, with the food and water feeling so heavy and prompting the sickness I wished never again to feel, that I wasn't going to eat again until I was truly hungry, nor quench a thirst that did not exist; for since The Rain first fell, it seemed I hadn't much a hunger or a thirst; that a sickness kept me alive.

The priest was still asleep when I opened the door to my brother's old bedroom. Bed sheets were covered in blood from his clothes. Peculiar, I thought, had the priest knelt by the woman inside the church? put his hands inside her chest? For his trouser legs were terribly covered in blood, his hands, his white shirt sleeves, even his clerical collar was not white but red! He was thinly, pale. I checked the wound of his upper left arm. It was red, sore. But no puss, no horrible discolouring of skin—no signs of a contagion; nothing visibly problematic.

His duffle bag was on the floor at the foot of the bed, where I had dropped it. But I noted that it had been opened, the zip evident with finger marks of blood. And it was still half open. As I bent down and began to unzip the bag the rest of the way, the priest stirred uncomfortably. I turned around, still crouched over the bag, to see him roll onto his side in a delirium of sweat. I opened the bag and found a change of clothes, a King James Bible, a hip flask, a wooden cross, and beneath all of that, I found a black dagger, large and with a roughly textured surface—which I took. There were no signs of blood to its metal, but I was suddenly suspicious of who this priest *really* was.

I left the room quietly, and, on my way back across the landing, I began to suddenly cough. My stomach filled, bubbling with a contracting pain, and I could taste rotten flesh upon my tongue. I dropped the priest's knife into the bowl of the washing basket lid and stumbled my way into the bathroom, awakening Rocky in the chaos. I spewed my guts up, like the time I had first lain in The Rain vomiting for the smell around me and in my nostrils. But this time, that same smell, that *taste*, was coming from inside me as I puked up my non-digested breakfast in spews of red, thick liquid. My throat stung so tremendously, my eyes cried, my stomach screamed and arms shook as I tried to hold myself over the toilet. I passed out quite quickly, and when I next awoke, someone I loved dearly was in grave and terrible danger.

#

The wind was at my back; wings beating currents of air downward. Columns of red engulfed the sky beneath, above and around me. I was looking for someone. I was circling a neighbourhood. My body felt so strong, my eyesight unmatchable. I came lower, falling through the air on gigantic wings. My feet touched down with a sound like metallic talons, upon a road flooded, flowing with The Rain. I could sense two people inside a house, they were fighting. I walked closer. I walked down their drive. Dogs were barking from inside the house. And then I recognised the house number, the front door, the front window, and the cars parked in the driveway beneath as I shot into the air on a gust of wind from the gigantic wings at my back.

It was my mother's house.

I awoke screaming and choking, laying on my bathroom floor, Rocky by my side barking into my face. It was just a dream it was just a dream, I thought erratically as I got to my feet and made my way downstairs and then out the front door. I locked the front door this time, leaving Rocky inside. I got in my father's Rover after quickly darting to open the garden gate, and I took off in a screech of tyres. Maybe they're still alive, I thought, maybe they're not dead, or infected, maybe what I saw.... And I began to think on what I had seen as I sped away from my father's house in my father's car into the afternoon sun.

I had been flying, peering through eyes that were not mine. It had been raining, and I'd felt so strong, so much control. The wings at my back, I thought, how, what, what creature had I accompanied. Even then as I hurtled down the road at an unprecedented, dangerous speed, I could not but feel the magnificent pull and weight of those wings at my back,—and then I saw the heart, which I'd left in my fridge, hanging by a string from my rear-view mirror.

Who put that there WHO moved the black heart WHO, I thought, my eyes stuck on the black flesh as it swung side to side, side to side. Had the priest awoken, had he found his knife on the washing basket lid. My mind drawn, impulsively, to the creature in my dreams, my foot pressed harder on the accelerator as I raced to discover the fate of my mother and my eldest brother. I'm coming, I thought, I'm coming. Forget the priest and his knife; the swinging heart, and the hands that put it there!

#

I rolled down the road with my engine turned off as I made the turn onto my mother's estate. The Rain had been pouring in my dream and when I arrived at where my mother lived, still pouring, though not as bad as it had been in my dream, but it was still raining. I spun my car around at the end of the street and pulled up outside my mother's home. Before I got out of the car, I felt a surge of panic. The creature I had witnessed, in my dream. I felt it above, watching. On the roof of my mother's house, maybe. I picked my katana up from the passenger seat, looked at the black heart beating, hanging from the rear-view mirror, blue veins luminous as it swung side to side, side to side.

    I stepped out into the road, The Rain pouring around me, my katana unsheathed, in my right hand. I walked onto my mother's drive, looking up at the house and then around at the neighbouring homes. Nothing, I thought, there's nothing here. No creature sat perched, watching from any rooftop. I looked up at the sky, and I saw no creature beating down with great wings over the columns of red rain. Then the sky flashed blue, I mean *electric blue*, somewhere in the distance. Lightening. I looked to the heart rocking side to side beneath my rear-view mirror. And it wasn't rocking anymore. It was pulling to one side, toward my mother's home, it's flesh throbbing and so radiantly webbed with blue veins I thought it might splatter against the car windows.

    I heard a barking come from inside my mother's house. And then the front door opened. "Who's there!" I shouted through the noise of the pouring rain. Before I could shout a second time, I noted a shadow stood silhouetted in the doorway. Long hair hung from the figure's head, she was looking directly at me. Mother, I thought. "Mother!" I blared.

"Get him," I heard from behind, and I turned around to see three figures running in unison, arms and hands raised to seize or harm me. I sliced through The Rain with my katana. It was hard to see, near impossible. But I felt my blade connect and I heard three severed heads fall to the ground and roll along my mother's drive. "Get him," I heard again, as if it came from The Rain, whispered by the columns of pouring red. And four more figures appeared close by, down the street. I walked out onto the road. They had come out from their homes, neighbours I had once known; they were holding variously shaped objects in their hands, from knifes to scissors to what looked like a cricket bat. "Get him," whispered The Rain, and I saw all around me front doors opening of the neighbouring homes.

A woman came hurtling at me with two pairs of scissors. I impaled her on my katana, raised one foot and kicked her to the ground, pulling my sword from her chest. Two more figures closed on me, their arms wrapping around me, holding me tight so I could not escape. I was dragged over to my mother's drive. I screamed all the while, the katana still in the grip of my hand, but I could not use it, I could not break free of the arms holding and dragging me away. They licked my ears as if to add extra anguish to my smouldered vehement. I both cringed and screamed.

My mother was stood in the doorway still, when the large figure from my dream lifted her up, high on wings into The Rain and with one strong twist and pull of its two arms, tore her body in half by the waist and threw her two sides into neighbouring front gardens. I was horrified. My heart beat so feebly and I felt the sickness again. The smell of rotten flesh festering in the air, suddenly. The creature landed gracefully on the roof of my mother's home, perching upon tiles as my hair was pulled back by the people now surrounding I and I was made to look and watch as it lifted up from the tiles of the roof a body I could only guess to be my eldest brother. In one clawed and large hand the creature held his body by the head. He laid my brother over his crouched legs and began to devour him. Or that is how it looked. I could not fully tell, as the beast's wings had come around some and shielded the ungodly sight from mine eyes.

Again, I heard the barking. My mother's dogs both came running from out the front door. I couldn't see them for The Rain and for the deranged lunatics crowding about me, holding me, forcing my eyes upward to watch the creature upon the roof as its head convulsed and wings shivered around its body and my eldest brother. And then I was set free, as quickly as I had heard our dogs barking and then running toward me. The crazed and infected holding me fell down, as my mother's pets leapt at them and caused the crowd to stumble and fall. "Grab him!" The creature screeched from the roof. I turned and made for my car and saw how surrounded I had in the street become. I sliced my katana through the air once, twice and a third time, parting several figures from their heads. I swung again, and again as I walked forwards, turning behind to swing at the crowd encroaching on my back. I opened the driver's door and got inside my car. I locked the doors and started the ignition, and as I did so I felt the roof slam with the meek weight of a body. My brother's

devoured corpse slid onto the front windscreen; and then
the beast descended upon my car, it's talons
horrendously screeching upon the roof.

My two dogs outside were already crying,
whimpering loudly in The Rain as I hit the accelerator
and took off, the creature sliding from my roof and
landing easily on the road. I saw my mother's dogs again
two days later, but for then I thought them surely dead.

#

Sleep, sleep, sleep. I could not, sleep. *...I aren't
able, aren't able....* These were as my thoughts the night
of February 25th, once I'd returned home in the dark by
few and little street lamps, and had rolled quietly into my
father's drive and secured myself in my bedroom.

Over and over I imagined the nightmare I had
awoken to. I willed myself to sleep, eventually. But over
and over, I was forced to remember the dream of soaring
through the skies as a high pitched whirring rang in my
ears; like a signal being broadcast.

As this signal stopped, in perfect synchronicity, I
was released from the waking realm and fell soundly
into the darkness of quiet slumber.

RADIO SIGNALS

Another note from my stalker. I awoke and the
earth was spinning, a high pitched whirring slowly
seeming to die, and, of course, the foul stench of The

Rain happened to be in my bedroom, window partly open. The bedroom door was locked, however.

I found a note outside, nailed to the garden tree. Before it caught my eyes, I was distracted by a standing heap of shining red armour. I approached the tree and the standing armour fell! The note read:

> 'I saw what the angel did to your family.
> You have a brother, still alive.
> Wear the armour; it is specially made.'

To my left, peering up from the grass, was a red, glimmering mask; a white waist sash; an armoured waist coat; tassets; greaves; everything to equip a samurai warrior, even, a red pair of fur shoes laid at the edge of the garden. The note was signed, 'Lu Tien Oloiv'.

#

Over the next week I got to know the priest. He told me about a brotherhood, and I thought him still delirious from tribulation. He eventually told me his name, after rambling about all sorts of peculiar things and beings. He told me to call him 'Lu'.

His memory seemed utterly perplexed; for all he ever spoke seemed on one side poetical and the other a riddle.

The note on the tree was right, because the same day I read it I pulled out my radio and began to search for a blip out there; quickly, a whole community emerged. They talked about the hoarse happenings where they lived, numbers of survivors, injuries. I shared with them my knowledge about the black hearts, the creature in The Rain, and the priest…. They told me of a nearby Garrison, based in Leeds, and they warned me not to go seeking my brother, but to wait for a message from York, staying put in Leeds. Apparently whole cities had been cleared, burnt pyramids of the deranged spotting the streets attesting to the work of survivors and the military alike. The military was scarce thin; it turned out 92% of the population had been infected by The Rain. No one made mention of the sickness I am experiencing, and frankly, I didn't feel comfortable sharing my symptoms from The Rain; it is the 9th of March as I now write, and in the last week I have had to make up my mind about a few things.

I'll briefly illustrate what has happened between the 26th of February and today, before I set out.

The priest, with his belongings, has fled me. A young adult, named Callum, has come into my company; he dresses like a girl to lessen the defence of a human adversary, and he acts like one too. At first, I thought him a girl, and then I caught him peeing stood up, while we were out on an excursion for supplies.

He came crawling out of bushes as I was driving down the M62; he ran out in front of me and nearly killed us both. I was speeding, and when I hit the breaks and swerved, the car did a sideway somersault and landed face forward, the right way up. I felt as though I sprained my neck, but other than that there were no injuries.

#

I've made my decision, and now, I'm heading out to find my brother. From one of few stable minds left to wander a God forsaken Earth, this is how the end came upon us.

THE FLIES

"When I close my eyes I see a great static; sometimes I feel as tho I stare into the abyss of space and can see stars both far and near. I wonder if I am dreaming, asleep somewhere; daily I wonder at this, for all I seem able to do is dream.

The days mean nothing to me, and with each passing night I feel I grow further into this *insanity*.

…Am I already dead?"

— From the diary of Jonathan Smith

I

Jonathan Smith hadn't the energy to climb out of bed early on a morning, or even late in the afternoon. His mind would swim tiredly and his knees shake and body ache dare he try to stand without premeditated effort and make for his bedroom door.

His father, being a scornful man—a father that one could only but endure through the grating course of a struggling coexistence—made Jon's life all the more harder. How his father's incessant judging would pour over him, tirelessly, when it was found that Jon had not been busy with his day. How his stone hard, analysing eyes would watch from their corners and scrutinise with deep wrinkles each breath and movement of Jonathan— be it so his father wasn't stinkingly drunk. And how his scalding, lecturing voice would drone on and on, like a buzzing noise monotonously haunting the air breathed by Jonathan Smith:

When are you going to make something of yourself, Jono? Speak up, boy. When I was your age I'd married your mother and gotten her pregnant. Put the kettle on, and another word and I won't have you in MY house. Buzz buzz buzz buzz buzz—like a pest, a malevolent insect of some kind, only stronger than Jonathan was, dominant over him within its own abode.

Jonathan Smith was trapped under his father's roof with no where to go, trapped like a fly in a spider's web—his father the spider, and his father's nature and words, his hate-filled love, the poison continually shot into Jonathan's veins. It is to no wonder that Jonathan Smith was so weakly every morning or afternoon that he awoke.

The front door had slammed shut moments ago, waking Jon from his afternoon slumber. Jonathan's father was surely home, slightly earlier than usual, and Jon was sat upstairs in his small and dingy bedroom, awaiting the bellow of his father's petulant voice.

Firstly, Jonathan knew that he would shout Jon to come down, and if for some reason Jon didn't hear him or didn't react quickly enough, it wouldn't be long until his father was marching up the stairs, repeating distastefully Jon's name with the last few steps of his assent. "Jonny, Jonny, Jonny," Jon would hear, proceeding a sharp rasp of knuckles at his bedroom door and then his father's impatient breathing on the other side. "Jonny boy. Oh, Jonny boy, open the fucking door," his father would whisper with a falsely kind air through the crack of Jonathan's bedroom door.

But his father hadn't called his name yet. Hadn't made a noise at all. Not a single sound had stirred downstairs since the slamming of the front door. Nothing. Nothing until, out of the silence, the stairs began to creak softly. Jonathan stood, filling with fear and scurrying clumsily to get dressed. Then he noticed, still half naked and through a haze of risen panic that had beseeched him so unkindly and without warning, the unlocked latch of his bedroom door, and with one quick glance he became horrified at the state and then the musky odour of his bedroom—he, himself, undressed and eyes watering and red from tiresome afternoon sleeping.

Awaiting the hoarse whisper of his father's voice through the crack of his bedroom door, panic and dread combined like poison to shoot through his limbs and turn him as weakly as an overgrown insect. And then a rasp came from the other side of the door, soft like the creaks on the stairs.

"Jonathan? Are you decent?" asked a voice, but before he could reply, his sister had swung open the bedroom door. Jonathan flopped down onto his bed, half embarrassed at the panic she'd caused him, half completely exhausted.

"Are you okay, Jon? You look awful!" she said.

"I'm fine, Ruby. I just thought... I thought you were dad is all."

"Oh, don't be silly. I'm not nearly as noisy as him."

"So… when is he home?" asked Jonathan as he shakily stood from his bed again, stretched wide his limbs and yawned.

"Oh, soon probably," she replied.

Jonathan stepped forward in his underwear, scratching himself, and his sister only just seemed to notice that he wasn't, in fact, decent. "Oh, Jonathan, get dressed," she giggled.

"I was about to until you just walked in, Ruby." He could see her better within the darkness that shrouded his doorway now that he'd stepped closer to her. She was wearing a wavy, white dress, her blonde hair was hanging loosely around her shoulders, and her pale face glowed with a delicate red about her cheeks as she chose to shy away her eyes from Jonathan's bare flesh.

"You know what he'll do if he catches you like this so late, Jon. Hurry… I doubt he'll be long from home," she said, the smiling glow of her face waning as she slowly pulled the door closed and left his room.

Jon listened for a moment to her steps and her soft descent back down the stairs, and let his posture slump into a more graceless stance and the little muscle he had—which he had been tensing slightly—relax now that she had left him alone in his bedroom. He loved his sister. She was the only person who truly cared about him. The only person who understood his situation, because she knew their father, knew of the violence and the draining spell of his being.

Jonathan turned to the mirror on the wall opposite his bedroom window and looked at himself. He was a taller, skinnier version of his father. The same long face, long arms and large but taut and bony hands. Hardly any muscle himself. More bone than anything. His skin was lifelessly pale, and his eyes small and bug-like.

He looked to the old and dust laden alarm clock laying on the floor by his bed and hoped with fear in his gut that his father would be home late. Moving to grab a pile of clothes strewn across his bedroom floor he stopped short, noticing the sudden stench of himself rising over the already musky air of his bedroom. He'd need to shower first, he realised. God, he thought, if he isn't late….

#

An hour past, and then another; and still, there was no sign of their father.

Jon had showered, dressed and made a half attempt to 'tidy' his bedroom, and had straightened up the house somewhat as his sister slowly wandered in a non-present state of some engulfing sadness about the house, and particularly the rooms Jon was in, without helping. Then he cleaned any messes their father might have left in his rush to get to work that morning. After feeding their two spaniels he'd left in the back garden all day, he took to the kitchen table by himself with a pot of coffee and a newspaper, flipped to the job titles near the back and left the paper open and unattended in front of him. It was an act. A disguise to deter his father. At least until questions were asked, that was. Jon wished everyday that he could wake earlier. Feel more energy. More motivation than to simply let the dogs out, feed them, and slump back into bed. But he couldn't. He half believed he was anaemic, and was half convinced that he was simply a 'lazy-good-for-nothing-bastard'.

And like that, as if on cue to the one floating thought of self pity, and as he was starting to become somewhat more comfortable and had begun to feel he could almost relax and half forget the lateness of his father's return home, heavy footsteps could be heard coming up the front drive. Keys rattled for a moment on the porch. And then with a sharp rattle of the door handle, the front door burst open. A draught of air spilt in and rushed across the kitchen, fluttering and partially tearing the pages of Jonathan's newspaper. The door thudded shut, and the grunts of his father were heard before the word 'Jonathan!' blared through the house.

Jonathan's heart began to palpitate again, as it had earlier when the stairs had creaked and his sister had appeared in his bedroom doorway. Then a hand, with a timid, cold touch, squeezed his shoulder gently, and his sister Ruby drifted around the table to sit opposite him. She cast him a brief smile before their father walked into the room.

"What are you smiling at, Jonathan?" snapped their father as he dropped his work bag onto the table next to Jon. He stunk of booze.

"Nothing…." replied Jon, dropping his gaze to the torn paper in front of him and fiddling with his coffee pot and cup to his right. He knew not to make eye contact. Knew the slightest tremble could provoke a confrontation. His best chance was to hold his breath, try not to notice the audacious reek of gin, not to make a comment, and, hopefully, slink off upstairs when the opportunity presented itself.

"Don't you spill that on my bag," his father slurred.

Almost a minute of silence elapsed whilst Jonathan's father made himself a cup of coffee. It was a silence Jon didn't tend to take for granted. He was quickly reading a few job titles before his father interjected with: "So...what's ol' Jonny boy been up t' t'day?"

"The usual, dad. Here, I made you a pot of coffee, if you want a refill."

"Did you? Ha.... well, why didn't you say so." His father poured away the coffee he'd made for himself down the kitchen sink and then drained Jon's coffee pot into his cup, spilling it drunkenly all the while. "Urghh, that's weak, Jonno. Make another one. Stronger, for God sake."

Jon stood up and moved with low eyes to the kettle, noticing at a glance as he went his sister's absence in the room. She must have snuck off when he was making his coffee, he thought, God, she's so silent. He filled the kettle and turned it on. When it came to a whistling end of steam he poured the water into the pot with twice as many spoons of coffee as last time.

"Better," said his father. "Now fuck off upstairs and take that old newspaper with you. You don't fool me. Fucker."

Jon walked upstairs, his father's eyes watching him all the while from the kitchen table whilst his large frame obnoxiously filled a chair, and his deep-set wrinkles lining his face beneath a wad of thinning grey hair strained to scowl under the brilliant light of the kitchen; Jon was grateful to get away from his father. Back in his bedroom, he slumped down onto his bed. Light from the setting sun broke through a gap in his curtains and partially illuminated the grimy darkness of his small room with a reddish glow. Meanwhile, from within her bedroom, he could hear his sister sobbing.

She'd been sobbing a lot recently. It's her boyfriend, Derrick, Jon thought. He'd been ringing the house phone lately, up until Jon's father had unplugged the line the other day. Even now, Jon could hear one of Ruby's old phones vibrating in the loft. She had so many. So many different numbers. And, God, they got everywhere. A lot of them seemed to be up there in the loft lately.

Jon knew not to ask. But he didn't need to. He knew what was happening. Their father had finally stopped her from seeing Derrick. He'd been confiscating her phones for weeks. Not allowing her to leave the house after late. At weekends. He'd slashed her car tyres twice. But finally, after not being able to get in touch with Ruby for a few days, Derrick had come to the house in his car late at night. He'd brayed on the front door for a solid two minutes. All the while Jon could hear his sister screaming at their father. Screaming and screaming—and almost pleading. And then, as the commotion seemed to simmer down and all that could be heard was Derrick's knocking and intermittent calls of "Ruby, Ruby! I know you're there," Ruby stuck her head out of her bedroom window and called down, "Go away. Derrick, just go, please. I don't want this. I don't want you here." And as Derrick had tried to interrupt, Ruby cut in with an almost whimpering cry of, "I don't love you, Derry. I don't...." But the knocking had persisted. Until Jon had heard a thud, and then a thump, and then something heavy break on the ground outside. He'd known his sister was throwing things out of her bedroom window.

After that, car tyres screeched outside and Ruby's sobs reached their pinnacle. Jon, at this point, finally dared to take a peek out of his bedroom door. But he slithered back inside, instantly, with an image that would shape forever and darken greatly the fear he held over his father. His father had been standing on the landing at the top of the stairs. He was motionless. A dark, looming figure shrouded in black. He was merely standing there. His long, muscular, ape-like arms tensed at his sides, his wide frame engulfing the top of the staircase. Machete in hand.

Jon was terrified. He'd hid under his quilts after scrambling silently across his bedroom floor, and tried not to listen to his sister's sobbing, her wretched cries for 'Derry'. But they had soon ended shortly anyway. After a slammed door and two or three heavy thuds, the house was quiet once again.

The next day, Jon's father had taken the day off work, which was odd—but what was even stranger was that even though Jon hadn't dared leave his bedroom all day, 'Jonathan!' hadn't been bellowed up the stairs—not once. This was three days ago. Ruby and their father hadn't spoken since.

In the back garden, overlooked by Jon's bedroom window, the rising barks of their two spaniels tore him from his thoughts. He'd put them out and fed them before his father had returned home, but he hadn't walked them yet; he had to be home for his father when he arrived back from work, or work then the pub.

The dogs broke into a chorus of whimpers, and loudly. They needed walking. I best take them out, he thought and made for the stairs as he heard the back door open and his father's swearing voice begin to scold the two of them. Jon didn't want him to drunkenly hit the dogs. It isn't their fault; they're only animals, Jon thought.

II

Jon's father had hardly noticed him when he brushed by to take the dogs out. He was too consumed in his anger to notice his son walking past. Jon was simply grateful he'd made it in time, as his father had been on the edge of the garden, almost a leg's swing away from the dogs.

Out on the field behind Jon's house, the dogs finally ran through through the grass. Jack Sparrow and Indiana Jones, the spaniel brothers. Jack had a tangle of black fur, indie of brown. And, together, they both dove freely like bouncing, wild crickets let off their leads amongst the high grass.

Jon walked behind them. He maintained a steady distance, allowed them to bound off, but called their names if they ever went too far out of sight. They were obedient dogs. Jon loved to walk them. He enjoyed being away from the house.

Once he had circled the field, taken a path through an archway of trees that stretched for about half a mile, and then taken a left turn back home, heading down a path flanked with high grass and bushes alike. All the while, amidst the short 'Hello's' he gave other dog-walkers, and under the thick heat of a grey sky and fading red sun, a set of thoughts festered in his mind.

The first was of his father and sister. Of their argument. Of what he saw and what it meant. He frightened him, his father, how he'd stood there in the dark with a machete in his right hand, his sister screaming at his side like a dying wreck. It was a thing of nightmares, and it had stirred many for Jon of late. Their relationship had always been strange, his sisters' and fathers'. She looked so much like their mother.

At first, their father had been loving. He'd managed after being left alone in the world as a single parent. But the years had dragged on him. The loss had burdened them all. And as those years did drag their father's mind down into a place of dark things, Jon's sister flourished, she flourished and she became more and more like *her*.

She was beautiful, their mother. They'd all depended on her in one way or another. Their father more so. And as Ruby grew up, and her face became so similar to their mother's, her sweet mannerisms too, her body, and everything else about her, she filled the house with an unspoken atmosphere. And it filled their father with something else; something entirely hideous.

A yearning had grown in his eyes. Jon had seen the signs. He'd wake up late in the night to use the bathroom and once or twice would notice doors open, creaks creaking in places they shouldn't. Those faint noises had told him a sick tale of their own. And his sister, she'd told him one too. Very quickly, the light in her eyes, that smile of her mother's, that way she was, had all changed. She became timid and frightful. Recluse and unheard. And their father, their father became brutish and hard.

Jon shivered fiercely as a splash of rain hit his face. The sky was darkening, and the clouds were beginning to give. About time too; it had been grey sky's and barely any sunlight for the last day and a half. He picked up his pace and let his mind continue to wander. He couldn't stop thinking.

I could have done something, he thought, back when I'd seen it happening. The signs. Oh, the fucking signs! Why didn't I ever tell someone—do something? Fuck. I'm sorry, Ruby. I'm sorry. He knew deep in his gut his feelings were true. Shit. Even he found himself drawn to her. She was beautiful. And the only female interaction more than a 'Hello' he was accustomed to. What a recluse he too had become himself. Secrets carry a burden, he thought. And burdens, they change people; they'll burry you if you let them.

It was his father and sister though who had changed most of all. They'd changed each other. Jon was almost unnoticeable standing to the one side of their downward spiral into the dark. He was as a mere spectator caught in some dangerous spider's web, watching from afar as the eight-legged beast reigned in and suckled its first victim.

Yes, his father ridiculed him, shouted at him, once or twice a week might have given him a good boot.

71

But it was those two who had felt the brunt of burdens. Look at him, he thought, my father, how fucking absent and drunkenly. Didn't even notice me when I brushed passed him in the garden. All that hate. God, the man had even forgot to put the bins out the other day... well... I guess it was the day after that night Derrick came around. What an unearthly night. And now the bins. You could say that was to become Jon's problem, see, his bedroom window rattled in the night winds because it wasn't properly sealed, and their was a vent above the window, to the left; the bins being directly below this point now meant that whatever food or crap was rotting in those festering bin bags would be all his delight. Shit, he thought, I'm going to need some air fresheners, remembering the huge collection of bin bags and their lumpy, unforgiving shapes sprawled in piles around the overflowing waste bin. *And the flies, fuck. The flies. There were so many when I left.*

Jack and Indie were sitting waiting for Jon when he looked up. They were panting by the bridge that crossed onto the fields, their fur coats damp due to the slowly progressing rain. It was time to take them home.

#

A dark feeling had followed Jon that late afternoon as he'd walked the dogs back over the bridge. It had started in the forest, high in the trees. A creaking that shouldn't have creaked on a windless afternoon. A feeling that had breathed within the dark heights of the path he had walked. And then in the long grass. He didn't notice it at the time; his mind had been too ajar with thoughts and regret. But it had followed him, a dark figure running in the grass behind him, like the wind, like a wild, monstrous cricket let lose and turned into something more evil than mere insect. Something foul and malevolent.

Only then did he notice the dark presence when he was finally across the bridge, Jack and Indie pulling him ravenously. He looked back over his shoulder and there it was; the suddenness of night; pitch black and with wooden arms jeering and waving hysterically up high in the trees to a windless evening that warranted nothing of the like. He'd been unaware how long the walk had taken him. Unaware of the building up of dark things around him and the absence of light as he'd wandered down a dark path of thoughts and had ended up back where he started, at the bridge.

Stark terror struck him as he stood there frozen, Jack and Indie pulling all the more wildly and whimpering as the rain advanced and that malignant feeling from within the forest latched its claws, too, into their wet furs and deeper. Until, like a strike of lightening, Jon regained his sense, and he rushed home out of the rain—not to look back once.

Of course, he wouldn't amuse the idea of his fancies once he'd arrived back home in the safety and comfort of his house. Instead, he brushed them off as tricks in the dark and silly little feelings of children, not knowing that the real threat, the real malignancy, resided within his own home. And that the feeling that had followed him back that night, quite simply, aside from the possibility of supernatural stirrings drawn to the macabre memories of Jonathan Smith, was the subconscious upheaval of a nightmarish kind of dread reassuring Jon its foothold within his misshapen life.

Once home, Jon dried the boys, Jack and Indie, down with the towels he'd laid out for their return. Shortly after he'd had a chance to consider and disregard the damnable fear he'd fled, and made sure the dogs wouldn't leave any footprints and that they were clean of grass and twigs that usually managed to latch to tangles of their furs, he then put them to sleep in the kitchen. They both laid under the kitchen table; as was their sleeping place. Jon turned off the light and gave the boys one final look, told them they were 'Good,' and finally let them alone in the dark.

Upstairs in his bedroom Jon noticed, instantly, the smell that had festered around his windowsill; and the flies, how a few had made it inside, through the vent above the window, and how they now flew back and forth into his window, as if in an attempt to escape the confines of his house. The windowpane rattled loosely in the winds, but only allowed the smell rising from the bin bags to pass through slightly. Most of all though, the smell came climbing, like the disgusting limb of some dead thing, through the vent above. It wasn't so bad that it was too abrupt over the air, nor even noticeably so over the already muskiness of his room. But if it wasn't for the rain, Jon believed, it would be much worse. The beginning of the week had seen a few days of high temperatures under a scorchingly cloudless sky, and more recently, the sky had been overcast with thick, grey clouds. The air was humid and it was hot. Like Jon believed, if it wasn't for the drizzling rain throughout the day, and the down pour in the afternoon, the smell would have festered terribly.

Of the few flies that had slipped into his room, one was still buzzing about between the slanted teeth of the vent. He looked to the one fly buzzing loudly and alone in the vent and ground his teeth at the repulsive drone of its existence. He'd need masking tape—and lots of it. Unless he wanted the swarm hovering over the rubbish pile below to find their way in too, to follow the echoes through the vent of the buzzing flies that had managed to leak with the smell and into his room.

After a few exhausting minutes of swatting the few flies that had made it inside, and taping up the vent with a layer of masking tape, Jon retired to his bed. He laid there, happy he was unable to smell the reek festering its carcass about his rattling window. Slowly, concealed and at ease with the dark of his room, Jon closed his eyes and allowed the dreams to come.

Behind the steering wheel of a car Jon found himself questioning the reality of his mind; though, other things seemed more urgent within his life. His face was slick with tears and the road in front was disappearing fast as his car sped along an open country lane. He felt tired. The passenger seat was littered with beer bottles, and he could feel he was severely intoxicated.

Everything moved fast. Too fast. He felt like he was in a runaway car heading for a sudden fate across the road.

Then a set of headlights came beaming into his rearview mirror. Rushing out of the dark of night like a malevolent wind. His heart began to palpitate; and he began to hear a voice whisper quietly from the backseat, rising like an echo over the air: "Jonnyyy," and then louder, "Jonny… oh, Jonnyyy…."

The headlights were close behind him now. Whoever it was wanted him off the road, and they were gaining. They went from tailgating to scrapping his rear bumper lightly and then ramming into him before Jon had the chance to shield his eyes from the blaze of headlights shinning, fiercely, into his car like projectiles of fire.

"JONNNNYYYY!" a voice bellowed from the backseat, and the wheels began to skid under the ramming weight of the car behind. Jon's car spun and began to slide, and then the car had flipped upside down, rolling, hurtling, bounding at high speed down the open road. His upturned car skidded, sparks screaming along each side of the vehicle. He came to a stop sixty feet down the road. Screeching tyres followed in the wake of Jon's wreckage. The other car pulled up beside him. A door opened and slammed shut.

Jon lifted his head to gaze out of the shattered windscreen. The world spun about him. He felt as though he was lying on the unearthly plane of another dimension, looking from out of the wreckage of his car and into a pitch black land of noisome buzzing.

—Buzzing?

A drone of sound filled the car: the wings of many meat flies fluttered, gushing like a chocking gasp of air, through the smashed windows of the car. Jon began to crawl. Glass cut his arms and hands as he went. And a stench gradually rose from within the car; he looked downwards to his lower half and the smell. What he saw made him wriggle in so crazily an attempt to escape the wreckage of the car that his arms and chest were soon covered in many deep gashes that oozed terribly with blood over the broken glass beneath him.

His trousers were torn severely. His lower half almost entirely naked. The flesh revealed below looked blackened, like charcoal. And where his male member should have been there was a gaping, black and crusted hole covered in flies, buzzing, entering and leaving in a cloud-like flurry. all over his legs Jon felt an itch, a fierce, scratching itch; he could feel it beneath his skin, like a rot eating his flesh from the inside out. He cried and screamed, crawling desperately out of the vehicle. The itch gradually filled him from head to toe, and a shrivelling feeling began to stretch across his flesh and pull it taut as a heat within his bones burnt intensely. He was sure his flaky skin might peel away in the softly blowing breeze of the night. The shards of glass were now unnoticeable beneath him as they buried sharp ends into his dry and taut flesh. Then, finally, with a push that sent him out into the cold night, the buzzing drone of flies ceased about him. He rolled over, gasping and feeling somewhat relieved and disorientated to have escaped the upturned wreckage of his car.

Heavy footsteps came walking toward him, one approaching figure illuminated in the fiery glow of a pair of headlights. Jon laid there on the hard, cold ground, gasping deeply; unable to move before a set of hands grabbed him and dragged his burnt and crippled body into the dark black of night.

As he'd laid there, half unconscious, the monstrous hands of some being dragging his crisped body to untold fates, he closed his eyes, like he had when he'd first fallen asleep, and the world and the dark and the cold sting of the night subdued around him; all suddenly becoming replaced with a warmth, and then a splash of water across his face. He was laying in his bed again. Morning light was beginning to filter through his window. The curtains had been pulled open and the window pulled up so that drops of rain had blown in and was pattering against his windowsill and one half of his face.

He was covered by his quilts and felt warm and at ease when a gentle rasp came at the door. And then a voice, quite like Ruby's, spoke softly to Jonathan.

"Jonathan? Are you awake?"

The door opened and his mother walked in. She was wrapped in a crimson night-gown and looked healthy and full of life. Her blonde hair shone angelically in the dim morning light. Jon tried to turn onto his side to see her, but he felt heavy and too succumbed with sleep. Sitting by his bed, she looked down at him disapprovingly through a faint smile.

"Did you leave that window open again, Jon?" She looked to the open window and back to Jon. "You'll catch a cold, you know." Rising slowly, she drifted over to the window to close it.

Please don't leave, Jon thought, unable to find his actual voice beneath the fog of sleep that rested above him. She ran a hand through his hair, "Get up whenever you like, I'll make you breakfast," she said. Jon found himself questioning the reality of his mind, and found himself hoping that all the nightmarish elements of his life and Ruby's had been a concoction of a dream as he lay there in bed—his mother alive, and his father most probably the man he once happily was. Then his mother strode briskly out of the room, her night gown drifting and flapping behind her as she went.

Jon tried to get up. He wanted to go after her. To hug her, to feel her embrace and soft, caring hands in his hair as he cried and confessed all the horrors of his nightmare. But he couldn't. There was a heavy weight like sleep upon his chest. And the more he tried to rise, the more he felt it crush him and he struggled to breathe.

His window began to rattle. The breeze outside was turning more violent and the rain was picking up. Then he noticed his vent taped up tightly with black masking tape. He began to worry. He yearned for the quiet footsteps of his mother's approach. The smell was already upon him though. The smell of something rotten. Something dying. And outside his window, the pattering drops of rain fell heavier and heavier; and gradually they turned black and froze still in the air, hovering; to Jon's horrified eyes, he saw the flutter of insect-wings becoming hideously apparent and real. Flies began to buzz against his single-paned window, the meat of their bodies bouncing like dead rain drops, back and forth.

A noise on the stairs suddenly intervened the maddening metamorphosis outside of Jon's window. He twisted his neck with wide eyes to face the half closed door of his bedroom. He'd only heard the distant sound of one faint step creak somewhere upon the stairs when the horror had struck him; a horror that could only follow such an unnaturally filthy metamorphosis, a horror that hid when the light was present and then came back with the dark, lurching in the victim's own fevered shadow. So, when Jon heard the second footstep sound softly at the top of the staircase, he desperately began to hope for his mother—but knew it could never be her again, not when the beast of his dreams lurked almost closely enough to peer with it's hideous smile from around the corner of the door. Jon knew that whatever form was to appear at his door, whatever kindly face may greet him, that it would soon shift that face to something horrible. But, nonetheless, he hoped, beyond sense, that it might be his mother if he could believe it over the approaching fear. He wanted to see her for one last time, visibly healthy and alive, his mother, a beacon of past light to fend away the coming dark.

Ruby appeared in the door way.

"Shhhhh. Jon. Stop making that racket, you'll wake him."

"*Jonnaaathaaann!*" he heard his mother distantly sing from the kitchen as the kettle rose with her voice.

Ruby walked in. And behind her, their father appeared, smiling, holding a cup to his lips. He approached the bed. Ruby looked on, worried. He looked younger, their father, less aged and less frayed, less tired. "Feeling lazy, are we, Jonno?" he said, and his smile seemed real, as far as Jonathan could see. His hand then felt warm, almost caring as he placed it upon Jon's forehead and combed back his hair with one direct stroke. "Oh my, you really could do with a shower," he commented, sniffing the air as he spoke. The smell was everywhere. Even Ruby looked to be holding her breath. Then his father pulled back the covers to reveal Jonathan's reeking lower half.

He was naked, and his skin burned, it itched and stung as he felt it drawing tight around his legs, as though burning under the sudden exposure to the air. Jonathan looked down at his legs, his breathing suffocating with the weight still upon his chest, and saw what he'd seen in the wreckage of the dream car: the black and crisp decay of his flesh. And then his father, with a slight smile, grabbed Jon's chin and turned his head to face him. "Jonno. Jonno. Be quiet now."

Jonathan tensed up as his father's monstrous hand came away from his chin. He felt his fingers venture across his crisp, tender legs and end, circling delicately, about a dry wound gaping between his legs. The penetrating feel of fingers pushed into Jonathan harshly, tearing his black, charred skin as they wriggled into the yawning hole of his wound. Jonathan's face swelled a deep red as he laid their, struggling in agony to the back and forth motion of his father's thick fingers. His sister looked on through horrified, vacant eyes.

Their father's face was hidden under a dark smile when Ruby came at him with a chair. The impact sent him reeling forward over Jon's bed; splinters of wood spraying in all directions. She dropped, with a heavy thud, the remains of the chair, and struck him again, and again, raining her fists heavily upon his head. Jonathan watched with intense eyes, not able to see Ruby for the enormous frame of their father. Ruby's impacts barely moved their father, and the strength and effort slowly drained from Ruby's attacks as an all-engulfing fear, like a black, vanquishing shadow had risen over her, drowned her might and replaced the terminal ferocity of her face with a picture of sickening dread. Their father rose from his sitting position and turned to face her. He pulled back his right arm, smiled again darkly, and in the dim morning light, a flash of steel shone with a dull shine in Jonathan's face as their father plunged the end of a machete deep into Ruby's chest. The noise of the house fell under a silence—breached only with the dead echo of splitting ribs, and then, momentarily, with the struggle of a dead girl's last remaining breaths.

Ruby's limp body collapsed, trailing a dark-red streak of blood, as if through a dream slowly, and landed on Jonathan laying terrified and shaking upon his bed.

Jonathan opened his eyes. He was covered in stickiness and sweat, and was breathing deep, harsh breaths; for the weight was still upon him. When he looked up he saw his sister rubbing her eyes and raising her head from his chest.

"Jonathan?" she whispered, "What's the matter?"

"What… what are you—doing? Why are you in my bed?"

"It's okay, Jonathan," she said. But Jonathan felt something weird in the way she had spoken. Something was strange, something was hanging around the air about her. It was almost seductive, alluring. Jon felt the caress of her bosom move against his chest as she laid there, half on top of him, her cleavage, Jon noticed, right beneath his chin.

Her eyes were still gazing at him when he noticed that his pants had been pulled down in his sleep. "You don't mind do you, Jonathan. If I sleep in your bed." She wriggled against him, her cleavage brimming slightly under his chin, her eyes smiling as though knowing of some pleasure.

"No. No. It's alright," he said, figuring by the desperateness of her clutch that she might really need him. He looked down tiredly. A shameful feeling was rising up in him slowly. It stirred in him more as she smiled back, and then, casually she moved her hand in a slow arc across his legs.

"Ruby?" he said, her nose tickling his neck now as she began to breathe steadily down his chest and look up. "Do—do you ever miss mum?" She looked at him flinchingly; a sudden coldness set under her skin, as though she'd heard the name of some frightful ghost.

"Yes. Things were...." she said, smiling through a frown-full expression. She rested her head down against Jon's chest without finishing her sentence. Her body ceased to move and fidget against his, and her cleavage seemed to retreat their seduction somewhat from beneath Jon's chin; her hand, however, had gone stiff with her arm as she'd begun to grope gently the bulge between Jon's legs and had heard the dreaded mention of their dead mother.

"Ruby?" Jon asked again as he felt himself becoming more aroused beneath her clutching hand. He didn't know what to say. He felt the need to comfort her, but felt uncomfortable himself, awkward with the way she made him feel. It wasn't natural; it felt desperate.

The heat began to, slowly, build between them again as Ruby's hand loosened and began to stroke gently his male member through the quilts. Jon could feel it. The smell of lust was rising as her slim body writhed against his, her breasts noticeably gleaming with a trickle of sweat. Then her breathing became long and hard; half moanful, half whiny, and growingly dirtier as her each breath crept and slithered steamily down Jon's unclad body.

As Ruby was getting slightly louder and the room began creaking under the faint movements of the bed, they both heard the fall of loud steps outside. Ruby froze still over Jon.

Fear held the two of them in a desperate clutch.

"It's pretty late Jonny…" she whispered. She was utterly quiet for a while, laying atop of him still and shaking coldly in the darkness of Jon's bedroom. A shiver crept into her words when she next spoke. "Jonathan please please. Don't wake him...."

The weight of sleep eventually returned to Jon's limbs as he lay there, straining to be carefully silent in the dark. His sister's hand was now unmoving, clutched against her own chest. And though the noise from outside still draped a fear of the unknown over them, the most unnerving thing about it was that Jon couldn't decide whether the noise had come from outside in the hallway, or from the outside beneath his bedroom window.

III

Jon awoke with morning's first light. Ruby was gone from his bed. He didn't know when she'd crept off but he had a feeling that she'd lain awake until the early hours of morning when she could be sure that their father had, beyond any fear of a doubt, fallen back to sleep and the threat of him catching her on the landing wouldn't be awaiting her as she swiftly crept back into her bedroom and closed, quietly, her bedroom door. Jon, however, had slipped into a deep and dreamless sleep, following the unknown thud which had startled and ceased their awkward late-night interaction.

As he laid in bed subdued with sleep, a dark and dreamless canvas hovering over him, consciousness had gradually approached his still body—like the sunrise stalking a distant point of darkness. The fears and the oddities he'd experienced the previous night, of his dreams, of the discomforting feel of Ruby's body, of the noise that had startled and unsettled him, all rose, slowly, to simmer for sometime beneath his dreamless state; until, with a sharp stroke, all the fears of that wretched night ceased the calm rest of his sleeping mind and dragged him up and into the world of waking. And so, the morning came upon Jon early for once, and, for once, he found himself widely awake.

At this point, Jon's eyes were quaking and wide open. He laid there still for sometime in his bed with nothing but the mess of stirring thoughts and his tangled bed sheets about him.

He was laying motionless, thinking deeply, considering the oddity of his life and the meanings of the darkly tied dreams he'd suffered that previous night. Something strange had followed him home last night, he could almost feel himself become more and more sure of it. Something had walked into his house. It was as though things had been stirred, startled into waking, as though a progression had begun through the unearthing of something unknown, something entirely malignant and corrupt. It wasn't inconceivable for Jon to feel the teasing of such thoughts and to even tease himself with the possibility of believing them. No. All things dark, after all, were seeming to come together, to pool, gradually, like dark waters filling an empty lake, the abode of Jonathan's fraying life.

Finally, after toying with thoughts, Jonathan got up and made to look out of his window. The day had begun blindingly bright and he had to shield his eyes from direct contact with the sun. He hadn't seen the morning's rays for sometime, and what he saw now could have burnt his pupils. The day was truly glorious when he got up and walked to the window—spoilt only when he noticed the faint stench still residing over his windowsill. It repulsed him and he stepped back. The tape was still sealed over the vent. No flies were in his room. And none, even, outside, buzzing by his window—which was a relief, considering his dreams, and the wake of heat rising with the morning—a heat surely to help fester the rot that sat in the ungainly shapes of large, distorted bin bags outside, on the patio below his window.

He turned to face into the gloom of his bedroom and slid down the lower half of the wall below the window to crouch on the floor. The disorder of his small bedroom sat illuminated in the morning light. Disorder, mess, he thought. Disorder, mess. Everywhere. Fuck this. Fuck them. Fuck. Ahh, fuck me. Fuck! Something… something's wrong… Jon's throat filled with a dry chuckle as he angled his head back to rest against the wall. He turned to look at his bedroom door. It was unlocked, the latch was out of place. He thought of Ruby. The way she makes him feel, the way she looks at him when she doesn't think he can see; and then last night, the way she'd touched him… Ruby, he thought solemnly. Ruby. So it wasn't a dream. You were in my bed last night; for Jon remembered locking the door before he'd retired, and now it stared, glaring back with the truth, unlocked.

A shadow came to fall over his small room and all the disjointed things laying across the floor. At once his room became dark. Black. He sat still, without noticing the absence of light shining in at his window. Sunlight cut away, his room became gradually cooler. And his thoughts, his thoughts of Ruby, they spoke ever-so-loud in his mind as he sat there. How suddenly he had confessed it to himself. The way he felt. The needs that grew upon her touch. He shivered in the dark setting that had befallen him, and began to notice the arousal suddenly creeping into his groin as the unspoken desires writhed under his skin like a disease suddenly able to fester. He was beginning to rub the bulge of his penis when he realised with clarity the oddity of darkness that had come to play about his small room; the chill; the cold impulse growing over him like a black stain. He stood up quickly, ashamedly, and as he did so the shadow fled his bedroom. Sunlight met his face and beamed like fire into his tired, squinting eyes as he looked to the brightness of the morning sky. Then that feeling rose again within his gut, the one he'd quarrelled with earlier whilst he'd laid awake in bed. There were no clouds in the sky, no trees with waving limbs, nothing high enough and close enough; no, nothing but perhaps the perch of some gigantic flying-thing could have possibly eclipsed for so long the sun. Yet a shadow had crouched over him and all his things. A shadow had looked in through the window, and then vanished. He rubbed his eyes. It's too early, he thought. Too fucking early.

The front door slammed shut. Jon stood still in the beaming morning light. He allowed the silence following the thud of the front door to wash over him before he looked to his alarm clock to see the time. Guess he's gone then, he thought.

The house slumbered in silence, from the landing outside Jon's room, through to the kitchen where the dogs were probably still sleeping; every molecule of air hung lazily throughout Jonathan's empty house when he left his bedroom and closed the door behind him. His father's bedroom door was closed. The bathroom door was left wide open and sunlight shone in, stretching an angelic finger across Ruby's closed bedroom door. All remained silent but for the creaking underfoot as Jon descended the stairs.

The light shining through the open bathroom door reached halfway down the stairs and then broke away in dark ridges of shadow. Jon reached the bottom of the stairs, finding himself standing by the front door, darkness all around. He opened the door to his left and walked into the front room. The kitchen door was closed. As he approached, he heard a quiet scuttling from the otherside and a table chair move and screech in the stillness. He opened the door.

The kitchen was bright. The dogs were coming out from under the table. There were no messes to be cleaned up, no spilt coffee or bread crumbs scattered across the worktop. Jack was limping. His right hind-leg dangled over the floor as he struggled to walk to Jon. It was nearing eight thirty A. M., Jon noted upon looking at the oven clock. He could feel the trembles still running through Jack, and Indie too when he came over wagging his tail and then curled up on the floor beneath him. They were both frightened but pleased to see Jon. It must be unusual to see him so early in the day. Normally he'd wake up around dinner, feed them and leave them out in the back garden. They both probably expected his father when they heard Jon coming through the house.

Jon opened the back door and let them out. Jack limped behind Indie as they both bounded out of the kitchen and into the fresh morning air. Light beamed in through the windows, gliding over the kitchen sink and the few dirty pots there, illuminating as it went columns of dust sat in near-stasis, but even the dust in the air seemed to shiver, like frightened particles unsure of themselves and the environment around them. Jon stared at the light and the drifting dust. Stared and thought, and then quivered. How the kitchen had never changed. Never been finished. How each particle of dust, stationary in the light of morning, were like that of his every memory—stationery, unmoving—of their lives within this one small, illuminated room.

The walls were a bright yellow. Unfinished. The paint just stopped and a pale, sickly green spread for over a third of the walls, the kitchen door centred to its hideous face. Why haven't I, or any of us, finished it for her, Jon thought. His mother had loved their kitchen. She'd seen so much in it. The table and chairs she bought, almost brand-new, from an old friend. Solid oak with a vintage appeal to their craftsmanship. And the vase on the windowsill, Victorian. Made of blue and white porcelain with beautiful dark-blue designs and multiple spouts. She'd only had chance to place a few roses in their but none more. Only had chance to paint most of the room but not all.

The dogs were outside barking. Jon tore himself away from the kitchen and walked into the back garden to find them both growling at the bin bags sprawled about the bin in unusual shapes. "Boys," he said, walking over to them. But they didn't move. Instead, they kept on barking, growling as if some thing was hiding amongst the rubbish. A rat, or whatever else. Jon moved closer and then had to step back and shield his face. The smell was putrid. But what he hadn't noticed was the swarm of flies buzzing in mass over the bags— until he'd half swallowed a mouthful of them and was now chocking, leaning over and retching harshly as he felt their filthy wings flutter meekly in his mouth and around his tonsils and a few terrified bodies tickle within his throat. He coughed hard. Swallowed. And then coughed again and spat. A few came out in the spit, but not near as many as he thought he could feel. He felt sick and staggered back to the the door, leaning against the frame with one hand.

"Boys!" he shouted, "Inside." He pointed and they both quit their snarling and ran into the kitchen to lay once more under the table Jon's mother had once bought. Jon felt his throat with one hand and massaged his trachea. His stomach was nauseous. He could taste vomit at the back of his mouth willing its way out. He swallowed the sickly feeling and instantly regretted it as he felt the dead body of a fly slide down his throat. He went inside and filled a glass with water. He took a mouthful, swished, gargled, spat, and then downed the rest to wash away the feeling of the mouthful of flies he had partially ingested, their fluttering wings and fidgeting little black legs, tickling and itching within his throat. He hung over the kitchen sink for the next few minutes. Waiting for it to come. And when it did, yellow and slimy and a putrid reminder of yesterday's dinner, it was speckled with the black spots of little dead bodies, some small, others meaty, but no flutter amongst them.

He drank more water, glass after glass until he could drink no more. Then he went outside, stomach now swishing and full of liquid. The flies were worse than he'd first glanced. There were so many. Swarms sat on the bags, others flew around the bags, some in and out of the bin at the back. All together though, they formed the mass of what could only be described as a fierce cloud of sickly, noisome buzzing.

Jon staggered tiredly into the garden and looked up at the sky. No clouds at all. No breeze. It's too hot, he thought. What could be in those waste bags? It reeks. It reeks like death. Like a foulness no living thing should smell. Ruby? He noticed the window shutting upstairs in the bathroom. She must be up, he thought and headed inside to find and bring her to the disgrace of garbage sprawled like the dismembered limbs of a decaying animal across the garden patio. But when he got upstairs and opened the bathroom door, she was not there. And when he went into her room to search for her, neither was she there. Not even the bed she sleeps upon seemed to have been touched. It was as if she hadn't been in the house at all; and Jon might have believed it himself had he not encountered her in his bed upon waking from terrible dreams last night.

Overwhelmed and scared—scared, he did not know why—, he turned to rummage through her room. She has to be somewhere maybe there's a note he thought as her closet creaked loudly when he began to open it (as though it hadn't been opened for some time). His hands left prints in a thick layer of dust where he placed them to slide the mirror doors open. "Ruby!" he called as the doors hit the end of their sliding rails and made a dull thud. Her clothes were all gone. "Ruby!" he called again, this time in a panic.

Her room was suddenly cold when he slid the mirror doors shut again. And then in the reflection he saw something. It was stood, meekly, behind him. He didn't register it until the door was fully shut and he'd began to turn around. Before he could react, before he could look again in the mirror to confirm the sighting of his peripheral vision, he was stood face to face with it. "Jonathan," it said, and he let out a terrified scream into his sister's face and fell backwards, knocking the collected dust into the air. "I am dead."

TO BE CONTINUED...

A GRAVE ENDING

Captain Roger shot down the road in a blur of blue flashing lights, unaware he was headed toward the beginning of what would grow into mass catastrophe, and the grave ending of all he knew.

His wristwatch ticked toward midnight. He and his partner Damien should have been heading back to the station to clock-out. But that wasn't an option. Not when at the last minute something crops up out of the dead of the night and you receive an urgent call relating to a domestic and an assault in a hamlet outside of town.

Everything about the night had been quiet, and racing now, to the scene of a suspected murder, that silence was deafening. One look to the streets and you felt it, the unearthly feeling rising with a midnight mist; from the blackness swallowing street corners, to the eerie flickering of faulty lampposts, the feeling was everywhere. Even the wind had grown into a sinister howling as they travelled to the call under a watchful midnight moon.

"The sooner we get this done, the sooner we can get home," said Damien.

"Yeah, the sooner the better—" Roger scowled, "—jeez, wish I hadn't promised the kids I'd take 'em to the seaside this weekend," he finished, remembering his promise regretfully.

"Ah, that sucks, pal. I'm sure this call will be nothing we can't handle, though. Be home soon enough and you'll be able to get some rest," said Damien, giving Roger that *don't-worry-smile* he so often gave.

Roger wasn't himself anymore. His marriage was reaching a bitter end. Slowly it grated on Damien, seeing his partner and friend in this state. He remembered how Roger had been on top of the world only but a month ago. He remembered that same happy man every day, and was disappointed each morning to greet the man who had taken his place, the man who complained, who wouldn't talk as much as stare away into space; the man with sunken eyes and a heart of mud—guess that's what a divorce will do to you though—most anyone, at least. And with the way it was going too, the threat of losing custody over his children looming bright, the sludge in his heart would have soon overwhelmed him to the grave.

The twenty minute drive to the hamlet bled with an unwelcoming sense; almost absolute as a strangely tempered isolation filled the front of the car, until an ambulance passed, charging away down a narrow road in a screaming hurry. The driver had looked crazed, his skin pallid and eyes wide, frenzied by a kind of petrifying madness.

They finally arrived and driving into the centre of the hamlet became encircled by six large and beautiful houses—the seventh, however, stood nothing alike to the rest with their trimmed hedges and planted gardens and painted doors—and the seventh their GPS pointed to. Roger parked outside the house. It was small, old and rickety, made of decaying wood. And every window glared with darkness. This was where the call had been made, and no one looked to be in, the front door half open. Roger killed the humming of the engine and turned to Damien, "This doesn't look right," he said.

"Don't worry. It'll be okay. If it's not, I'll just score a hat-trick and save your ass for a third time," Damien laughed—yet Roger could see the doubt surrounding that *don't-worry-smile* of his, beside the lame reference.

Grimacing, Roger swung his car door open and rose from his seat. He walked to the front of the garden. Shining the beam of his flashlight upon the property, and he grimaced broader: every plank of the wooden house looked diseased, and the garden, void of all life, invited no one, only perhaps the like of gravestones to match its decaying stench, dead wildlife and forbiddance echoed in the darkened eyes of crumbling stone gnomes. The beam of Damien's flash light came to Roger's side, rescuing him from a deathly feeling he couldn't quite apprehend.

"Wow. Spoooky!" mocked Damien, until he smelt the stench and his stomach began to heave. "What the HELL is that reek?"

"A bad batch of horse manure, maybe," explained Roger. He raised the beam of his torch, picking out an old stable to the left of the house. It was only small, but four horses had managed to be cramped in there together, three as black as night, and one as pale as a corpse with deep-red eyes.

Somehow, those eyes mesmerised him with their liquid-touch of blood, their hard-ruby stare. He felt utterly drawn.

The three black horses had the look of skeletons as their skins hugged tight against their ribs. Callously,

96

they barged each other, attacking the front gate of the stable with their hooves as they reared and kicked, all neighing hoarsely, their jaws snapping ravenously at the air. "What the heck are they doing?!" asked Damien in an alarmed tone. "How have they even got the energy to do that?" he asked, even more confused. "It looks as if they want to—want to eat us!"

"They look almost rabid." Roger shrugged. Damien broke from the stare of the pale horse and tried to take the lead to the front door. He took one step forward in front of Roger, and Roger grabbed Damien's shoulder, pulling him back with a sudden jerk. "Look!" Roger said in a serious tone. And they both looked to the ground where Roger pointed.

Dark-red foot prints trailed the garden path.

"Is that blood?" Damien asked, his voice void of mockery.

"Pull your gun out," Roger ordered as he drew his own and pulled his walkie-talkie out, sequentially.

"We're going to need back-up at number seven, Stick's Passing. Urgently! Over," Roger calmly shouted into the receiver of the walkie-talkie.

And without waiting for a response from the precinct, or Roger, Damien shot ahead again, arrogantly taking the lead down the path. Roger's legs yearned to run home to his children, but he couldn't... his eldest had headed into a house draped by omens.

"Wait, Damien!" called Roger, ignoring the muffled response from the precinct.

Damien shone his flash light through the half open door; the house was an abyss of dark shadows, and no life stirred—but for one dim flicker coming from the kitchen. "It's the police! We've had a complaint of domestic abuse on the premises, is anyone home?" he shouted into the emptiness.

A shuffling noise came from down the corridor. Then suddenly a shadow lurched into a flicker of life under that one dim light.

"Someone's there," said Damien to Roger as he abruptly entered, once again surpassing Roger. He quickly walked down the hallway to the kitchen, turning twice to check the two doors he passed. Gun raised. Flash light blaring. "Hello?" he called just before he reached the dim lighting.

Roger rushed to keep up with Damien as he made his way forward. "Not so fast, Damien," he said as he reached the doorway under Damien stood. His gun raised. He looked to Damien. "Damien," he said, almost like an order. Though Damien didn't answer….

And then Roger saw it: the horror flashing across Damien's face as flickers of light jumped on and off him. His *don't-worry-smile* was drenched in disbelief. "What is it?" asked Roger.

A small girl stood in the middle of the kitchen under the swinging glare of a dim ceiling light. Her face was hidden as she stared at the floor. She shuffled now and then in a twitch-like fashion, flexing small, sharp fingers. She was surrounded in a puddle, her feet squelching as she twitched, in a puddle of swirling, black-red blood.

Roger noticed her bare heart as it faintly beat in her chest. Her rib cage was wide open and half missing; she looked like an open book of organs and intestines all dripping with blood.

Roger fell back and caught himself on the door. The girl's head snapped upwards. Her eyes a pure, bright white as they saw Roger. She was frothing violently from her mouth when she came at him. Running like a possessed puppet she reached out with claw-like fingers. Roger raised his gun. He couldn't fire. His mind succumbed to horror as he thought of his own children. She fell to his feet just as her jaw came gnashing at his stomach. Damien had unloaded a shot straight through her skull. She twitched dead by Roger's feet in an engulfing sea of blood.

"What just happened?!" Damien shouted under his breath in a petrifying state of madness. His eyes met Roger's. But he wasn't there. Roger was lost in his own horrific shock, staring into the gaping hole winking with gore in the back of the little girl's head. "ROGER! Pull yourself together," Damien cried.

Then a harsh *thud* fell on their ears and drew the dizziness of their attention upstairs.

Roger's eyes flickered back to consciousness. "Upstairs," he whispered. But before he could move, Damien was already flying up the staircase. Roger climbed to his feet and stumbled after him in a panic. Screaming came from one of the bedrooms, ceasing as instantly as it had sounded.

Damien and Roger burst into the master bedroom, together.

A woman laid on the floor next to a double bed. Her neck was bruised with the marks of fingers. Her mouth hung open in a ghastly O; silently crying for mercy. Her face was pale white and looked harder than petrified wood. Damien dropped to his knees beside her, hopefully, yet pointlessly, checking for a pulse.

"Careful! What are you doing, Damien? She might be possessed… like the girl, who came at us with her rib cage half o-open…"

"Well, what can we do? Shoot a dead person, and then check for their pulse?"

Before Roger could reply, the woman's eyes snapped open and that familiar bright white glared at Damien with a dark possession of life.

Her corpse shocked into animation as she gasped for breath; then her arms clawed and gripped Damien, her head rising to his neck, snapping. And she snapped with an insidious hunger and tore through Damien's jugular with one clean yet savage bite.

Damien pulled back and rammed his gun into her mouth. With an exploding roar, her brains splattered the carpet.

Roger fell to Damien's aid, catching him in his arms. Damien spluttered and choked on his own blood, lashing his head from side to side. His neck poured with the colour red whilst Roger tried to apply pressure to the wound.

A new panic ran at Roger; a bombard of steps coming from the doorway of an en-suite at Roger's back. Thick fingers clasped his neck and lifted him from the floor with an inhuman-like strength, like a bolt of lightening had ceased him and raised him into the air.

The woman's husband choked Roger in a death-like grip, slamming him into a wall, Roger's feet kicking feebly the air.

Her husband had the same whiteness swimming in his eyes; a possessed glare staring from the depth of the soul. Then the man's blood-covered teeth yawned in Roger's face.

Roger brought the mouth of his pistol to the man's chest. He pulled the trigger twice. The man stumbled back, dropping Roger on his feet. The man screamed with a hoarse, frothing cry like a rabid animal as he made to cease Roger again.

One bullet to the eye and the man went down; the white glare vanquishing as he fell to the ground in a heap.

Roger had no time to think. The sight of his partner dying on the floor in a growing pool of blood immediately turned him toward sane action. He swung Damien over his right shoulder and fled the room, cascading down the stairs, heedless as he slipped on trails of blood. Raising his right foot, he kicked the front door open into a blinding bolt of light.

The abyss of the house shriveled around him and he stumbled into the night air beneath a great and luminous moon.

Every front door to each house in the hamlet no longer stood sealed, but wide open in their own snarling grins of a dark nature, blinding white eyes watching from each their contained abyss; watching intently the rider mounted upon the corpse-pale horse centre of the encircling hamlet.

The horse reared and neighed under the reigns of the rider; they both looked so compatible, sharing they the same haunted, glaring blood-red eyes. But the rider wasn't deathly pale, no, he was an ominous black blur hidden in a dark-green cloak. They moved closer to he then, the bright, white eyes shuffling from darkened doorways.

The white-eyed villagers moved quicker and quicker toward their hooded master. He raised what looked to be a scythe in the air, and his horse again reared, whining loudly. The residents saw Roger. And their shuffling turned to stumbling sprints as they then made for him.

Roger scurried down the garden path from the house, carrying Damien over one shoulder, leaving a thick trail of blood as he ran. He popped two shots through the night air and they cracked like thunderous whips into the nearest skulls of the glaring and deranged white-eyed folk of the hamlet. As Roger made to open the passenger door, a little boy lurched out from behind the patrol car. Roger raised his gun instinctually, stark horror grew in his eyes as he sobbed, and he let another pop hurl from his gun. Another down.

The other villagers were too close though, five of them only feet away from his car. He began raining the remains of his clip into them, one by one, until a whirling siren broke into the hamlet. Thank God, he thought. Backup.

Roger flopped Damien into the passenger seat as the other police car skidded to a stop.

He jumped into his own seat, and with a twist of the ignition, brought the car engine roaring back to life. Backup was shouting with guns pointed at the hooded figure as again it raised its scythe and the white-eyed villagers turned from Roger's car to the men in blue having just entered the scene.

Without hesitation, Roger hit the gas and fled the hamlet, his tyres screeching and siren howling away.

They met the main road, Roger picked up the radio and screamed for help as calmly as his state of hysteria would allow. But no voice returned. Only the voice of dead static breathed back. And through the rear-view mirror, he couldn't see the other police car or the men, nor could he hear any gun shots. All he could see was that pale horse and its hooded rider staring back at him. Blood-red eyes in a green cloak of darkness.

He drove onwards toward the city and away from that dreaded hamlet. Those blood-red eyes burnt in his mind like fire, and those white, those pure, bright, white eyes!... and the little girl, her organs hanging on display until she had lain on the floor in a sea of blood... finally that woman, that woman who laid dead, strangled; his soon to be ex-wife haunting her pale, mercy-crying face with her own.

Tears brimmed his eyes and he felt his soul draining away from him, his skin growing slimy. The horrors behind him swam through his thoughts and his mind ached with the fear of tomorrow. A fear for his family.

He picked up his mobile and dialed home. It seemed to ring forever.

"Hello?" a little girl's voice finally answered.

"Baby, is that you?"

"Daddy! When you gonna be home?"

"Soon, sweetie, soon. I'm on my way. Is everything okay?"

"Yeah, I guess. But I think there's something wrong with mommy."

"What do you mean, baby?" Roger asked, his heart bleeding with panic.

"She went outside with the garbage and hasn't come back in. I heard her at the door. She couldn't open it, Daddy. She's scaring me. She keeps knocking really, really loud, Daddy."

"Just stay inside, sweetie. Look after your little brother and stay inside. Don't let mom in. I'll be home in a minute. Stay. Inside."

The phone cut off.

#

Roger entered the city. The streets surrounded him with chaos. Chaos were alive; cars laid abandoned in the middle of the road, fires burnt fiercely and billowing black smoke choked the city air. He passed corpses of men and women, of dogs and cats, of little boys and little girls; the streets were truly spilled with blood, painted red. But hope still glowed in the eyes of civilians as they saw his police car, though, only did they turn bright-white and glow with anger as he left them to their fates.

He turned onto the street he lived, which would have seemed untouched by the madness of the city, if it wasn't for the stench of death or the screams rising over the night. Or the sound of his wife, braying hysterically on their front door.

"Wait here, son, I'll come back for you," he said to Damien, squeezing his shoulder. But Damien didn't respond, his eyes were shut and his skin pale and cold.

Roger couldn't bring himself to think of the worst, so he'd just squeezed him, and promised him it'd be alright.

He swung the door open and jumped out. "I'm coming, baby," he whispered to himself as he ran across the road.

From the edge of his garden path, he could see his wife. She was knocking on the front door as if drunk and had lost her keys. "Honey? Susan?" he called.

She turned around. Her face was pale white and her nightie was stained with what could have been wine. Her eyes glowing. "Oh, God, no." Roger stumbled back. She shuffled toward him. His arm raised his gun. He couldn't. It was his wife, yeah, they'd had their problems, but it was his wife, the mother of his children... and he still loved her like the day they first met.

She stumbled forward, momentum giving her speed. He had to make a decision. Her hands came clawing in, jaw snapping; utterly unhinged, eyes consumed by a darkly glowing white.

He pulled the trigger.

"Daddy!" a voice screamed from inside the house.

"It's okay, baby!" He ran towards the front door, opened it and rushed through.

In the middle of the hallway under dim lighting stood his children, both shivering in each others arms, both sobbing hysterically. "Daddy!" they cried and cried.

"It's going to be okay, guys. I'm here," he said, and hugged them both.

"Where's mommy?" his little boy asked.

Roger brushed his boy's hair back, and he said, "She's just gone—gone out, kiddo." He paused and hugged them both tight. "We'll see her again, don't worry."

"Are we still going to the seaside, Daddy? You promised this time," the little girl asked, looking up and smiling.

"Of course we are, baby."

Roger's gun felt heavy in his holster as he pondered over what to do. He knew there was no hope, but he couldn't let his kids be killed by those... those things. He couldn't let them die at savage hands.

"Ice-cream and sandcastles?" his little girl asked.

"Of course." He squeezed them both again.

"What's wrong, Daddy? Why are you crying?"

"Nothing, princess. I just realised how much I love you both, is all."

"We love you too, Daddy, don't be silly!"

"Daddy?" his little boy asked.

"Yeah, kiddo?"

"Uncle Damien's here!"

Please God no... Roger turned around, holding his children close. Damien was slouched against the open doorway. He looked delirious, pale, and when he smiled his *don't-worry-smile* Roger picked up his children and backed away, his gun in its holster suddenly with a weight he knew that he could not lift.

Damien's eyes were glowing, and the neighing of four horses pitched loudly over the distant cries of the burning city.

FREDERICK GOOLE

PROLOGUE

This is the tale of my entrapment, of how a boy named Frederick stole my heart (and I don't mean in the romantic way, either). My heart is no longer where it should be. He removed it while I was spectral, you see. Spectral?... What on earth do I mean.

I will tell you what I mean... better yet, come and see.

—Casey

PART I

"Give it here, Sam!"

I sighed. Since Sam had brought that toy train of his out to play Steve and Rick hadn't stopped in trying to pry and trick it from his whining, little hands.

"No! It's min', you gickers," screeched Sam.

A smile crept across Steve's face and he laughed, Rick chuckling behind him ever-the-louder, ever-the-deeper. "Am a what, Sam?" Steve's head pressed close to Sam's and lent sideways. Sam turned away. They'd been teaching him new swears all day and Sam didn't know what-meant-what anymore only that they wanted his toy train—which they weren't getting, at all.

That was when Sam quietly began muttering to himself, "It's min', not having it, nobody having it. Min' min' min' min'…" Sam knew, however, despite his efforts and protest, that Steve would trick it from his hands or pry it, eventually, away, as had he all other toys Sam had brought out to play. So Sam sulked, grounding the little red toy train in the muck, as if it were the cause of all his suffering. (Sam was only four, and I hated to see Steve and Rick prey on him like this.)

The boys made the only sound for miles as the brick and mortar houses of our cul-de-sac village slumbered, clouds floated along the sky white and mysterious, and rusty-orange sunlight hammered down on the golden cornfield where we played.

When I saw him coming, through a stasis-like gap in the waving, tall, yellow corn, my heart sank, and I dropped my gaze to the ground, and hurried over to Sam. It wasn't often he left his home, once or twice I'd seen him talk with Steve and Rick from his front porch, Frederick Goole. In some ways he's kinda like Sam, I thought. Frederick Goole even seemed of a similar age, perhaps a year younger by look; his demeanour, his voice, however, had, for the brief moment we had once known him, seemed ageless; I knew what it meant that he had come out of his home. I knew the tricks Steve and Rick would play. They'd cause a scene, the horror that would ensue… words hurled, rocks thrown. I knew that I wouldn't know how to dispose of myself afterward, when the guilt comes creeping in. I was the only one possessed with a sense of shame for what Steve and Rick had done to Goole.

Saddest thing was, I believe, Frederick Goole only wanted friends he could call his own. But that couldn't be, for what he did to Steve and Rick, how he corrupted them. I don't know if he meant to do it, but... sometimes, sometimes I felt no shame when I thought about Goole, and sometimes it haunted me and I would wake in my bed with a melody of laughter ringing through my ears.

Frederick had been unusual. He introduced himself to us one day, announcing that his parents died long ago without him, and that he had been alone until we had knocked on his front door.—Even though we had run.

He had said many a curious and stark things to us, in fact, so many strange happenings passed from his lips as we (I, Steve and Rick) walked with him that day; I believe he somehow crippled the minds of the boys; and it was only with that thought that I could retain the illusion that my two friends had not turned wholly evil but were warped unto a forgetfulness, that their personalities had taken on mutilated forms, siphoned remnants of the spirits that Frederick, in hushed tones, had so keenly spoken of; that the tales of lost souls and wandering cripples absent the flesh of mankind had entered Steve's and Rick's heads, taken tangible forms to them and began to fester, to conduct and subvert reality from them, to sear with a hot iron their moralities; unveiling to them powers and laughter, evil for the heart's content; grand foolishness; delusion.

Even then, as I peered up at Steve and Rick to see if yet they had noticed the approaching figure of Frederick Goole, I could see it plain in their eyes, and by the sharp points, like invisible hooks, pulling tight the corners of their ever-grinning mouths.

Rick's chuckles echoed like the terror-inducing chimes of some far away air-raid siren; while Steve's cackling, quieter and more highly-pitched, seemed to strike and reduce with strangely symphonic tones Sam to a crying, pathetic form upon his back, like a miserable blue beetle waiting for a predator to scrape out its insides and chow down. And it was as so, that nobody other than myself had noticed Goole approaching. Rick's dark-green eyes glared down at Sam like black dread, whilst Steve's, bright white about cold-blue irises, were nonetheless startling,—like high wattage, artificial lighting possessed his countenance: making you quiver, and the most uneasy feelings come over you (as though cold, dead hands had reached into the cavity of your chest, to feel the roundness of your beating heart).

Even now as I remember this, I feel the weight of my heart, absent my chest as it is, caressed in the cold hands come through Steve's entrancing glare.

Goole drifted closer across the cornfield, his grimy, ink-black curtains of hair swinging side to side, revealing the indented, crooked mass of his forehead. Winds from the south gradually picked up speed until they burst across the corns toward Goole, and the gently swaying figure of Frederick seemed to jump and skip, as if both having stumbled and leapt in one stride. He was a small yet ungainly boy, pitifully gaunt, and younger, I believed, than us all but Sam.—Only I saw that Goole was dead.

I shifted uncomfortably sat amongst the tall, waving corns, and my heart squirmed up to my throat as dared not I make an utterance of terror as the approaching corpse, that I believe to be the living memory of Frederick Goole, gained ever closer, ever unnoticed. I gulped and my fears turned to Sam.

Sam had been dropped on us by his mother. New to our village and in some rush, she had decided to leave him with us, thinking that the children who played outside her home were both immediate friends and babysitter to her four-year-old child. She'd been away all day, and I'd done my best to know Sam, hell!, for his sake, I'd even bullied him myself, that he might go home. But he hadn't left. He had stayed with us all day, running his red train through muddy patches between corns as Steve and Rick hovered about him, like vultures, teaching him words that weren't real and mocking him when against them he used their vocabulary, stealing they his every other toy his hands could not watch over or hold until he had no toys left and he ran home and returned with the favoured train.

Steve spotted Goole before he came too close, and it relieved me to see the figure of Frederick stop. As though to an old friend, Steve shouted, "And what are you doing out here, Goole! you old wretch."

Goole's black hair clung heavily to his grey face, eyes peering through the curtains thereof. His black pupils stared, how they stared, and vacantly, at us all. Blood-shot and quivering, Goole's gaze darted from me, to Rick, to Steve, to Sam, and finally rested on the little red train playing in the muck. His eyes slipped back behind the curtains of his hair, retreating into tight sockets beneath an indented mass of forehead, and an unnerving squelch and pop carried on the wind. I shivered, sharp, unholy tingles rising up my spine, and it felt as though both Steve's and Rick's glare were suddenly pressed upon I, and Goole's eyes, set deep in their sockets, from behind greasy curtains of black hair, searched the pockets of my conscience.

"Catch, freak!" Steve blared as he slung a brick in Goole's direction. It whirled against a gentle wind, spiralled down in a beautiful twirl of orange and red, and with a sharp and jagged corner sliced Goole's cheek open—and seemed, almost, to bounce off of him. Goole was unabashed, he didn't move, in fact, he hardly registered the blow at all or the open wound and tears of blood spilling down his grey face.

Sam bolted at Goole. Something I hadn't expected. I clawed at the air, trying to stop him. But he had caught me off guard. "No, Sam, STOP. Leave Frederick alone!"

Sam ignored my cries.

I believe Sam had only wanted to impress the boys, but I cannot be sure. The boys, after all, had been filling Sam's head all day, muttering to him as I'd half tried to keep my distance. I didn't like to get too close to the boys, see, when they were squawking, for I fancied I could hear voices that weren't there. I had once tried to stay away from them, to not play out on my street anymore, but then voices, and so many, lost, flittered through my dreams. And I half fancied, even then, as Sam ran away and I cried for him to come back, that Steve and Rick weren't making any noise at all but something was cackling, quietly, in a background I could not place.

And so there Sam went, running and swinging his little toy train in the air after Goole, his orange head of hair almost invisible in the rusty-golden sunlight as it mixed with the colours of corn. Goole turned to flee the second Sam bolted at him, his ungainly frame both seeming to crawl and drift over the field at once, like a pale mist with bobbing head and swaying black hair, and he faded from sight through the corns as the winds lessened.

"Don' wun, you scaredy gick!" Sam cried from afar, and then was gone… the corn stopped moving, and all that was in my eyes as I looked about for Sam was the sunlight and the silent yellow of the corn. The boys hurried ahead of me to the edge of the field. I followed them and made it just in time to watch Sam disappear once more from sight, vanishing into Goole's old house. I had tried to cry when I saw Sam climb up Goole's front porch, but no sound emerged from my throat. A hopelessness clawed at me evermore when my chocked voice finally did emerge, and I wailed at the boys: "Go get him! Go get him!" I could feel the blackened windows of Goole's home pressing into my mind, keeping secrets and many voices at bay; streams of noise hidden therein, awake; unseen glimmers peeking.

"Okay, but we're getting eggs, first," laughed Steve.

"No, Steve, don't!" I cried, but they didn't listen. Steve and Rick left me alone in front of Goole's old house. And it wasn't voices in my head or come from the dark that lured me through the front door, or anything beguiling or evil, it was fear that when Sam's mother returned for him he wouldn't be there.

Front door half open, sunlight pouring in from the porch, the rays dying in a dark emptiness, I entered Goole's abode. "Hello?" I called, but only my voice came in reply, bouncing from high walls.

I tip-toed. Darkness was everywhere. Moving figures shades yet darker stared from the walls, from the ceiling and from large cobwebs that plastered the walls, old furniture, and every corner my eyes could define. Please come back Sam, please see sense, I thought. A giggling rose from a door leading down to the basement. My spine came alive with fright and the darkness on the walls seemed to leap and glare, and jumping through the open door downward to the basement, in a frenzy I confronted the giggling. "Sam!" I shouted. I scrambled down the stairs, peering all the while. "Sam?" I was walking into a giggling darkness and Frederick Goole was the culprit; and there he was, sitting cross-legged, running a broken toy train along a cold, stone floor. Goole had removed the toy's wheels, and the underneath scratched loudly as he ran it back and forth, drawing, as though with sharp crayons, the floor in faint lines of red.

I staggered when he stopped playing with the train and his giggling grew louder, and then my voice escaped my throat and I harassed him, hysterically, "What have you done with him? Goole!"

Goole gazed up. His eyes peeking through darkness and greasy, black curtains of hair, he seemed to smile at me; a blood-curdling smile, a smile which bore teeth and loosed a playful tongue. "Goole!" I screamed at him a final time, and I became breathless. That was when he stood and his giggling ceased.

His shoulders, how they slouched, and his back, how it hunched, how he seemed so aged in the darkness, and for his unusual gangly smallness, suddenly he was tall!; the toy train, broken, lay across his white, upturned and outstretched hands.

"Why don't you come and play with me?" Goole cackled in tones of decrepitude. His laughter flooded me, and all I could do as his figure rose into the air, suspended like a puppet on malevolent strings, was shake terribly until he swept forward; until his black pupils filled with a void all I saw; mechanical tones of his laughter ringing between my ears as I awoke in my bed, terrified, drenched in perspiration.

Yes... a dream. Well, that's what I had hoped for until I found Sam's toy train under my pillow; absent wheels.

PART II

My parents taught me many things; about the wars; about the bible. But not about little boys who play where it is dark. Not about Goole. The abandoned farm house where Goole lived was never spoken of. We, as children, had asked. But not a word. And I couldn't go to them now, they'd have thought me silly. I should have told them about Sam earlier that day, before I woke up in my bed. I was afraid, in fact, that they'd take away Sam's train if I told them now, and then I wouldn't have had anything to prove it to myself. Sam's mother never came back.

We will get straight to it. Fredrick's house was a home of the unseen and, shortly, I became one of them.

When I awoke the next day, after barely being able to sleep, outside my bedroom window were Steve and Rick, a head of blond hair and a head of black. They were grinning, as always. And Sam was with them. Even, he was grinning. Sam. That's when Steve hurled an egg and it splattered across the window pane. Sam didn't ask me any questions, following when I got outside to them, dressed, and went with them. I didn't know where we were heading, but we went into the cornfield. Sam's face was pale, pale as Steve's and Rick's, pale as Goole and those he… infected. They weren't paying attention to me as I walked with them. Occasionally, I caught a glance from either Steve or Rick, and saw the laughter in their eyes.

Sam had been full of questions yesterday, when he realised I wasn't mean and before the boys became too heavy on him. He finally asked one half a mile into the corn, and it frightened me,—not the question, but how he asked it. "Which way do you want to go, Casey?" I hadn't seen his lips move, his eyes glance or head turn, nothing changed from the moment before Sam spoke to the moment following. And there I was again, walking after them as they all grinned, Steve and Rick throwing me stray glances, Sam, vacant and uncurious in their midst. Then the question came again, through Sam's gritted teeth, "Which way shall we go, Casey?"

They stopped, but none of them turned, Rick and Steve merely peered over their left shoulders at me, staring from the corners of their eyes. Sam, stood in their midst, eventually drew a long yawn and said into his chest as he lie curled on the ground, "Let's stop here. I think it's going to rain." Rick and Steve followed suit, and, before I knew it, it was raining, and heavy. Steve and Rick lay in the corns, like Sam. The rain was only getting heavier and I didn't know which way to look: at them, the sky, or Sam's train in my hands.

"Won't you play with me?" says the familiar, strange voice of Fredrick Goole from behind my right ear; I didn't feel anything sudden, but the rain stopped after that and the sun's light became blotted out.

"Play with me," I hear echo against walls in darkness. My first thought is that I'm in Goole's house again, in the basement. "Won't you play?" 'No,' I scream in my mind. 'No,' I try to scream aloud, but I haven't a voice. "Can't speak? cat got your tongue?" laughs Goole.

I didn't know I was in a cage, but then a door in front of me swings open, and I lean forward and grab metal bars, and I hear him again, but he's outside the room I'm in, ahead, beyond another wall. "Come and play," he calls. I scramble upright and tread toward his voice. There's an open door ahead. I can't see it for all the dark, but his voice comes through a space, like a doorway.

I stepped through and the air changed, the room and darkness at my back were gone, and the darkness that was ahead became filled with the light of the sun and a blue sky. There was a lake in front of me, but Goole was nowhere.

I sat down on steps leading to the edge of the lake, covered in a shade by trees and bushes. There's an island of tall trees in the middle of the lake, I notice. The ground is an orange lay of dirt and small rocks under my feet, and in the lake, just outside of shade, I see a wasp drowning on its back, it's wings submerged, its legs kicking all ways. There's nothing around me but silence, when I hear Sam's train playing in the dirt three steps down to my right. Sam is sat two steps down. And either he just appeared, like some figment, or I, carelessly, did not see him there.

"Sam?" I ask, but the boy doesn't turn around. "Sam?" He continues to run his red train through the dirt. "Sam?" And I remember then I haven't a voice. But I am speaking now, I thought, puzzled. Aren't I?...

The wasp finds its legs and stands on the edge of the lake. Somehow it managed to climb out the water. It cannot fly yet, its wings are too heavy. "Sam?" I ask again, but this time I made the distinction and I don't hear my voice externally, because it's in my head. I lean forward and touch his shoulder, but he moves away. Sam walks to the edge of the lake, leaving his train to lay in the orange dirt behind. 'Sam!' I wail. 'Sam!' I'm standing now, and Sam is leaning close to the water, he's crouched down and is running his fingers over the surface. How filthy, I think; the lake is murky, brown and orange and yellow, the sunlight giving brightness to a multitude of rubbish atop the surface.

The wasp flies past my face. I stand. 'Goole!' I scream in my mind.

"Let's play," whispers Goole in my right ear, and then I'm pushed forward and I tumble down the steps into Sam; and into the lake we fall, Goole on our back.

I wake up in the corn. Right where Sam, Steve and Rick had lain. I'm soaking wet. There's no one around.

When I ran home I greeted my parents in hysterics, wailing at them,—because now I had a voice to wail with,—and I told them everything, about Sam, about Goole, about Steve and Rick. Only, I had no broken, red train to show. Only, they didn't believe me. They were awful worried. They phoned the doctors that evening.

#

I went back looking for the train, into the cornfield. I couldn't find it; I couldn't find them. Fredrick's house stared at me as I left the corn and the sun bowed its head into the horizon. Someone was inside that house, looking, with vacant eyes, through blackened windows. They were all inside.

"Casey! Casey!" I heard my parents calling. They were walking down the street when I saw them, and I ran over to them, and I cried, and I told them where they're hiding, Goole and the boys. I told them they're inside his house. But they didn't respond, they but carried me home and put me to bed.

I checked under my pillow five times that night for Sam's train.

"Poor Casey, come down with the flu again," I heard them saying downstairs. The doctor had examined me and it didn't do well for my case.

"Your child is experiencing mild-to-severe flu symptoms," the doctor told them, like he knew.—I had surely come down with something, however. I'd been hot and feverish all night.

"Frederick Goole has my friends!" I had screamed at him. He didn't seem to hear.

I wasn't going anywhere that day, as far as my parents were concerned. Albeit, I was rather ill: so maybe I shouldn't have gone looking at all... maybe if I'd have listened to them I wouldn't be in this mess; my heart in a jar. I'm forced to watch it beat upon my windowsill at night. It only appears at night. During the day it is not there, but at night it appears and it glows a dim red, and pulses for me to listen. They've locked me in my room now, so I can't leave when it's quiet in the day—even my walks do not go unsupervised. I dare not tell them about my heart, that I don't have one in me, for I fear they will send me away (and Frederick wouldn't forgive them for that).

To this day Goole taunts me, and Steve, and Rick, and Sam, and all the shades of darkness that live in that house. Outside my window on a night and early on a morning before the neighbourhood wakes, they gather and crow my name.

PART III

Pigeons clamber in the gutter over my window. Steve and Rick have disappeared. The boys hadn't shown outside my house for three consecutive mornings, of the time to I allude, instead pigeons fought and cooed and flapped their wings in the gutter above my window, awakening me on the morn. The fourth morning that to the pigeons I awoke however, I dreamt about them, the boys. Sam, Steve, Rick, in the corn, their heads all filled with dirt; I could tell because it was coming out their ears.

I went walking early that day following the dream. The pigeons stopped flapping their wings and fighting and cooing and grew still, watching as I left. I felt them following me in the sky, a few moments later. It wasn't until deep in the corn that I heard a coo. The morning bright, I saw clearly ahead through the corn in all directions, far and wide, and I noticed wherefrom the cooing came, and quite immediately. Sam stood on my far right, plainly among the corn. And without delay, I felt the presence of both Steve and Rick, for their shadows reached past me and my back grew pale with horror. And like a vapour, I vanished from that scene.

#

Goole had me. He had me from the beginning when we knocked on his door, when they let him in with his words, and his brother… I haven't told you yet about Frederick's brother. His brother is silent. I was currently in their basement.

This is where I appeared, as though through smoke, coughing, unsure of where I were. And so, there I stood, in the basement. Only, things were strange, even with all that had seemed to happen: for I was no longer solid, and the shadows were no longer flat.

Goole had taken me this time, fully and without doubt. I wasn't going to be waking up in my bed, I felt.

And then I saw, as many a dark presence surrounded me, the bars of the cage; only the bars did not remain but the shades did.

We are there now, the place I have spoken of, where the glimmer's peaking reside, in Goole's abode, a place where you're not meant to see: the place unseen.

You may see something glimmer through the blackened windows of his family's home, but you will not find where I was kept, nor the cage, nor the lake, nor the boys, nor any place or any thing therein I shall describe. This is the place unseen.

The first shade that illuminated itself to me had a pretty face. It was rare. The shades, their faces I had seen as I lived in Goole's abode. Many faces, many shades. But none had such a pretty face as this, none had grown yet bright before me to clearly see.

I weren't sure after a while if it were shade or person as I gazed upon it. Of course, I knew it was a shade, for it had in the darkness of Goole's home drifted by me, and then turned, and surrounded me in vapour grey, revealing the twisted, black smoke of a figure contorting. And then with light, its face.

It were truly neither shade or person, but both in one. It spoke to me, and told me a tale, and vanished back into the darkness of Goole's home.

It's face was purple, with red cheeks, blue eyes, golden hair. When the Shade whispered, for it did not speak loudly, its voice was as a gently humming bird's, and its sentences were distant, far apart, far-off.

ENVIDIA

Into the hands of Zoul fall the foul and conceited, those who become a garish image of what first the Creator made them by their deeds and thoughts and a growing darkness of the heart. Envidia was one such person as this; and the Creator, whose name shall not be uttered in this manuscript, gave him up to the wretched caress of Zoul, God of the Damned, Keeper of the many fragmentally abiding gaols that wander beneath your feet and on arid, lonesome nights when phantoms can be heard to cry from a place undetectable and in-between the normal wavelengths of hearing and rise to the heavens for a brevity, in false hope that they should escape the confines of Zoul and be reunited with the Creator.

Envidia would have lifted his head to look around was it not that he was cast in the ground, an ugly head sitting atop a rich and peculiar soil. This is where the accursed Envidia now resides; surrounded by cabbages of the most large and splendid leafs; he, a green sprout upon the soil, his body buried like a hidden stem, limbs like roots extending wildly under this patch of earth whither Zoul has placed him. He grows the more amiable characteristics that were once his when the Creator first sculpted him from the clay of a terraqueous plane floating within the island universe of Madriphur; or so he is told, that he is kept, by Zoul, to his betterment, and that each passing of an age or an aeon sees him a fractal closer.

The head of Envidia is aware that he is not growing at all, however. He is aware of the unchangeable nature of his being upon that rich earth, the molecular density of his face and neck and shoulders being close to that of stone; only his limbs retain sensible flexibility and the capability to feel, extending they, his arms, legs and digits, in great and fanciful spirals under the soil in that Envidia is kept and that upon grow cabbages of a most unmistakably beautiful, effulgent make-up.

Can Envidia see the patch of greens in that it is he 'grows', why, no, of course he can't. His face and neck and shoulders are all made of stone, and only upwards can he see! Into the starry heaven Zoul hath cast overhead, Envidia gazes with a twisted expression, his mouth grimacing a set of small, grey teeth, irreducibly enraged with envy, veins once throbbing are permanently enlarged across his temples. Ever since his untimely fate and rebirth in the grasp of Zoul has Envidia endured this lasting state, spying as far as Zoul would allow his eyes into the starry heaven, observing nebulas of radiant purple swim far-off through a great darkness between the distant constellations of Madriphur. The haunting and spectral form of Zoul intermittently flashed and glared down on Envidia, and the constant babble of his mind would become ceased, and Zoul would gaze resplendently with either golden or purple eyes, and Envidia would hear the voice of Zoul heave over him, a kind of mockery and sermon intertwined.

No, not could Envidia see where he dwelt but gaze heavenward. Indeed, he was aware of his body buried beneath soil, and the growing of his limbs and digits like great tangles of infinitely weaving roots travelling through a vastness of soil that aeons could never give registry to the end thereof.

His stony countenance was covered in a dense and effulgent moss, so that his head, neck and shoulders and the hood of his monastic robes he donned now and in his previous life were alike to the splendid green leaves of the cabbage patch that Zoul had so planted Envidia within. And when too he had been formed within this one of many confinements of Zoul, he was shaped with such an expression as with which he had died. His right eye was closed and his facial features bent to the left; a purple stamp, like that of a tiny face, mimicking his countenance, impressed in the centre of his forehead.

LARRY THE LIZARD AND THE LORDS OF TURMOIL AND MADNESS

INTRODUCTION

Maya Metropolis shuddered an unseen shudder; as the denizens slept; as the government adjourned sector, S. N. A. K. E., scoured the labyrinth of sewers beneath that fine and upstanding city. Their documentation was kept private, unauthorised even for to be graced by the eyes of the King, regarding their search for 'Larry the Lizard'; the fiend suspected to have for untold millennia plagued The State: a creature identified and singularly-recognisable by the *strange* descriptions afforded he.

There is no simple way to disseminate to a populace the delusional and, to all appearances, macabre truth of Larry; and so, all rhetoric, the hysteria that proceeded when Larry was deemed to be real, has been hushed, and the denizens of poor, subjected Maya led to believe that Larry is no more than a man; a man whom resides amongst them; a man of a sure bent, maniacal, depraved and irreparably-deranged suit.

Though, what S. N. A. K. E. did not deign to share with populace or King is that they were searching not for the man whom had fallen under Larry's 'possession' (as they so put it), but for that entrance that leads to Larry's world and birthplace; that primordial sod; a place wherewith they desired to harness dark and unbecoming powers—to protect the world from itself, of course.

This is the second book of Larry the Lizard, and if you are faint of heart, *turn back now*.

PART I

Andrea, Detective Superintendent, of the private sector S. N. A. K E., stood perplexed and bewitched as she stared into what she knew not to be the very gate Larry had used in transmuting from the world Andrea believed in to the world Andrea did not. Alas, she stood *more* bewitched *than* perplexed; her bewilderment but a part in the enchanting allure of ineffable conveyances that a Room of Glimmering begets the mind. And presently, as five Detective Inspectors stood about her, aghast at the shimmering sights and wailing cries and the noise of gnashing teeth falling through the darkness that hangs from the corners of this room which they had stumbled upon in labyrinth depths of Maya's sewer system, and after crawling through an extremely narrow tunnel (whence Inspector Veronica had first cried aloud in spotting a grey, illuminate haze hopping away); Andrea, with her long, blonde hair swaying in a hypnotised, ticking fashion, her ears rushing with the sound of forthcoming rising water, strode slowly to the lip of the Black Lake and left the Detective Inspectors under the sky-blue vines of a willow tree (a tree that none of them but she had seemed to see).

"Andrea!" they beckoned, but Andrea was not in control of herself—Larry's Queen spake quiet words under the ambiance of the Room of Glimmering to Andrea—and Andrea couldn't help herself not to stride into the black waters, for the seduction and power in the Queen's silken voice, and the friendly hop of a silver hare that, to Andrea's eyes only, had hopped without a splash or a sound across the dark waters which seemed to extend beyond the confines of rationality; a sea where a sea should not exist.

The Inspector Detectives spoke for hours, rapt by a glowing gloom, upon a bed of moss in that room under the city of Maya. Andrea had simply stepped into the water and sunk, like a block of concrete. Quickly, a diving team was brought to her aid, but they vanished, never to return to the surface of the lake or sea, whichever it is. Word was sent to Nigel G. Winttahouws; and henceforth, a group of scientists have been positioned in the room that is being said to glimmer with strange lights from within a perpetual darkness.

Hours passed as the Detective Inspectors marvelled and talked at length about what they could see and hear, until the willow tree appeared before *their* eyes, and the sky-blue vines started to swing through that air which is like a glowing mist to the trained eye, and a tormenting vapour to the untrained; they hurriedly left back through the narrow tunnel, for the vines of the willow were surely trying to capture them, they thought.

"Is it me, or does this tunnel look so narrow that one should scarcely fit through it, yet here we all are, of differing width and girth, managing to pass through, and the struggle is the same for each of us, and *none* of us considered ourselves able to climb through?" asked Frederick to the other Detective Inspectors.

"You're right, Freddie," replied Annabel as she awkwardly climbed out the end of the tunnel. "I hope Andrea is ok," Annabel wept into the shoulder of the nearest of her colleagues once they were all through the tunnel.

But Andrea is not okay; those of you who have read the first book (*The Path of Bone*) shall know: without a pearl, or an accompanying Goddess, not a man, or a lizard, or beast of any kind, survives the descent, transition between worlds (even one equipped with gills); not being able to properly transmute, one shall either drown or ever find themselves sinking downward, never to rise, never to find birth in the waters of the Primordial Womb, that sea in the underworld of Larry's kind.

#

"They won't touch this," said Nigel Winttahouws to Towu, his Felis Catus (a short-haired Persian cat, with a stripy white-sandy coat and green-ish yellow eyes). "They act as though they have all-power, S. N. A. K. E., but really the King won't be grieved to give them His time; won't tie Himself to these unfortunate circumstance that have malignantly entangled us all."

"Meow," replied Towu.

"Yes, Towu. *Meow.* ...I'm only an Officer, Towu; yet here I am, the head of this... this... sardonic cacophony, delusional investigation. And here *we* are Towu. In Larry's office. Why? Because S. N. A. K. E. has asked us."

Larry's office was cordoned with yellow tape, as was the whole car showroom. The fresh smell of polished floors and new cars felt like a distant dream, to be there; a total depredation, of that lambent-atmosphere supported by the farcical desires for things *flashy, new* and *over-priced,* had occurred (this in the ensuing ambrosia of fantastical talk regarding a man-eating lizard, or a deranged salesmen able to infer spasmodically obscure thoughts, sights and feelings into them that were subject to his close-proximity and existence); and such an existence it was, that no trace had been uncovered of Larry, his whereabouts or person.

Eldritch, the only word peculiar enough to describe this office, thought Nigel to himself as he played with a taciturn biro and red paperback notebook found on Larry's desk and looked from the ceiling and walls to the floor. The flooring, reflective-grey and pale-white, molluscan tiles, (utterly obscure, for they—the tiles—appeared like hands of shells), and the *desk* and *drawers*, (of which held many a woman's unclean garments covered in a green slime), were not bought in any retailer across Maya or The State beyond; but seemed to belong to the crude craftsmanship of an improperly trained carpenter; boasting the grey-brown, rough and fissured tree bark of the elm. The walls were dark-purple; and a lightbulb hung from the ceiling without shade or fitting.

"Meow," coughed Towu the short-haired Persian cat as the oaken door of Larry's office swung open, and in entered the five Detective Inspectors followed by a man whom called himself the Chief Constable of S. N. A. K. E.. He was garbed in a long, yellow dress-coat and wore a hoary moustache in need of a good trim.

"Maya Metropolis is under attack," the Chief Constable quietly announced as he closed the door to Larry's office behind him.

"How do you mean?" asked Nigel.

"We... we stumbled upon something," answered the Detective Inspector Sam, an elderly man with long hairs on the tip of a broad and lumpy nose. "We don't know what it is, only that it glimmers, and is very dark, that there is a surface of water, a bed of moss, an' a mist that at first goes unnoticed but then becomes torturous, lest you study it carefully; and lastly, an obscure willow."

"You seem extraordinarily calm, Detective, despite what you just described and the nervousness of the situation," Nigel retorted.

"I always am. They call me Still Sam, if you must know. Not everyone feels the way I do, however. And Maya Metropolis is certainly under 'attack'. At 5 A. M. this morning an unnoticed shudder was recorded on instruments fine enough to detect such events; and since our discovery of this... room, within Maya's sewage network, excrement and all the vile materials that pass through those tunnels and pipes, and the creatures that scurry and sleep therein, have been bubbling over, onto the streets. Maya is under attack. Larry is nowhere to be found. And a mysterious women has forced us to block all visual media outlets for her unwanted, incessant and frightening appearances on the screens."

"And what can I do?" Commanding Chief and Officer, Nigel G. Winttahouws, asked. "I who am acting on behalf of my superiors. I in the light whilst all others quiver in darkness."

"She has asked to meet with you, this woman. You cannot refuse. Besides, she is *very* beautiful."

#

The day was spry over Maya despite the long-drawn investigation led by S. N. A. K. E.. The sun was high and hot, the birds were chirping, but the denizens were not: they felt low, and cold, and chirped not one bit. Sewage had frothed up from the gutters and manholes and made the whole city of Maya STINK.

Nigel went to meet this woman, whom has been said to be *very* beautiful, and he was most surprised when he saw her; for she wore a crown, on which was adorned seven white pearls; and she had the most marvellous purple eyes; yet before he could become bewitched by her beauty, he noticed the one thing others had not: a strange little man with green skin, seated upon a chariot harnessed to two parrots.

It hovered about her head, this *thing*, and with a bow made of a sugarcane and a string of honeybees it shot five flowery arrows toward Nigel (one white, one orange, one yellow and one blue), but he ducked and each one missed him.

They were in the Room of Glimmering, and alone she had requested that they meet. By now you might have noticed that this women is the Queen of lizards, of the 'world beneath many surfaces', and so we shall capitalise Her 'Her', and refer to Her as Her Majesty (for let us not upset Her).

Affrighted, Nigel hid behind the willow upon that mossy, green bed. The Queen, ever-so-enraged that Nigel hadn't been pricked by any one of Her arrows, ordered Nigel to come out from behind the willow, and he did. Her voice had been suddenly like a man's when She had spoke and commanded Nigel to stand before Her. Nigel, stepping out into Her sight, wrapped himself in the willow's sky-blue vines, but the tree began to wiggle and shook him out into the open and glowing darkness of the Room of Glimmering. He could not see the Queen then, for the air which holds like a lambent mist became torturous and clouded his eyes. "Hush, hush," spoke the Queen as Nigel began weeping, and groping through the air for something to hold onto. "There, there," said the Queen as Nigel's hands found Her bosom. But Nigel pulled back, and splurted in disgust.

"What is this?" said the Queen in outrage. "Still none of your arrows have pricked him?" Nigel was quite concerned by this point, and the air was beginning to treat his sight more kindly as he studied what couldn't be seen, and he saw again that tiny green-skinned man, and his chariot and two parrots, and a horrible-looking woman with a slimy body, daemonic purple eyes and a silver crown of black pearls.

"What are you?" cried Nigel as he made to squeeze out the tunnel which leads to the Room of Glimmering.

#

"She's beautiful!" cried the townsmen and townswomen of Maya Metropolis. "She's wondrous!" they roared. "She's divine!" they wept.

All but for the one Nigel Winttahouws were raptured in the rays of Her splendour. All but for Nigel Winttahouws, the whole city of Maya had gone mad; frenzied with admiration; blissfully filled with a love so intoxicating none could smell, see, feel the faecal rivers rushing along the once clean and upstanding streets of their cherished Metropolis. What would become of them? as Her Highness glided between them, risen from that mysterious place between underworlds, stark-naked, a tempest of lustre—of such beatitude, that in concordance, the whole of Maya were at once Her's, enslaved, enraptured, endeared.

But not Nigel. He saw the *sliminess* of Her body, the ugliness that loathed to break free from beneath Her shinning flesh—the wicked glinting of Her eyes—the foul smell of Her beauty.

The reciprocity of The State had always been fair across lands under their rule and analogous with them; the people of Maya, however, were treated with the kind of pomposity associated to royalty or highly-esteemed religious figures (except, of course, in the depredation ensuing the fallout-whispering of a one, mysterious Larry the Lizard; eyes and ears and tongues became most ungracious toward thriving old Maya then), for to live in Maya was considered a privilege, and a virtue, and, frankly, a *very* wanted position in the world: that they had allowed Larry to dwell among them, that they hadn't seen through his lizard scales, or had strong enough moral grounding to not be influenced by the swirling yellows of his eyes, bode unwell for them and positively bloomed in the charade put forth now by the Queen. She had espied them in the waters of a very private chamber, wherein lies a one, carefully cared for man that She has fallen hopelessly in love with. The State, King and all His royal council, kinsmen, bishops and archbishops, would have nothing to do with Maya since it became, by word of mouth, hearsay, unsolicited reporting, and a general hysteria that could be seen upon the dripping brows and strained faces of orthodox news presenters, the epicentre of a hellish-delirium. Such this emergence of Her Majesty was what The State and King had feared the most, and was the perfect way for the people of Maya Metropolis to expose the Phantom from the Past.

This Phantom I now tell you of is what underlay the foundation, secluded itself in the crevices between the bricks and beneath the pillars of Maya: the travesty of darkness that came before the Metropolis was formed, the Kali Yuga, the time and culmination of derangement, mindless, senseless, sense-enthralled Wrathadom.— From this period emerged the tail-spin of reformation, the slow and gradual direction upward of mankind's virtue, and sprung the four noble traits of the denizens of Maya Metropolis; which are, *none-violence, none-indulgence, servitude,* and a *willingness* to die for King.

Larry had lived in the Kali Yuga, and had upon the Aquifer acquired the lightening rod of his power, a dark possession which had bled into his soul so that to this day he saw all citizens of Maya as the damned and delinquent beings of the Past Phantom, the memory of that old time in which the mind of man was engrossed in only material life.

Larry could be said to have on his head, like the head wears a hat, a *cursed* mind. Divinely cursed we would come to see, for the ghost of his actions, that memory of them, the reality they possessed upon the waking, physical plane (a dreaming-oddness and nothing more or less), would make the Larry we know into the Larry we've yet to behold. If one beheld the behemoth city of Maya, they would see a fanciful delirium playing out, and the awful, smiling character of that detestable lizard killing with unseen hands the happy occupants of this citizenship.

The Mayor of Maya Metropolis stepped forward, to stand in front of Her Majesty, from the swarming assembly gathered therearound Her, and he proposed to give Her a bouquet of flowers, and these flowers were four *beautiful women* happily tied together—the most beautiful women in all of the Metropolis. This was when Larry spied the scene, and he thought, They're trying to trick her!

Suddenly, all the citizens looked wicked to him, a slight darkness around the eyes, anything that would be ugly to him, and that great Phantom pressed over their heads and Larry became very afraid and everything seemed dark and he was uncertain for the safety of his Queen.

Larry hadn't needed to follow Her Majesty up through the sewer, the Primordial Sea or the Room of Glimmering, for wherever She went he could appear.

And likewise he had done so, emitting into the ether from out one of the seven pearls atop Her crowned head.

Nigel noticed Larry then. Nigel was under the darkness that hovered about the denizens, in-between the people, and he crept away from the scene of ensnarement beneath the Phantom of the Past, and bravely he strode up to Larry to pull on his suit sleeve.

"My dear friend, I see it too," said Nigel. Larry was most surprised, for he thought himself invisible.

"Can you *see* me?" asked Larry.

"Yes. I have witnessed the fantastical creature that projects itself onto you. And that is not you. It is a dream of God." Larry couldn't bear to look Nigel in the eyes. Larry turned away and wept bitterly. In a moment Larry was gone and a man stood before Nigel, a normal man with a white face and a gruff beard, blue eyes and a meek smile.

#

Nigel had realised his opportunity to cease the degradation of Larry's self-ensnarement and the calamity wreaked by he throughout the Metropolis and the world's thereabout, analogous.

The answer would be slight; that thing to pervade the shell of Larry and bring peace to the enclaves of his being that had warred for untold millennia, and until Nigel spied him, a man upon the Surface of which Larry had been ordained by that power imbued by he upon the Aquifer to wreak havoc, seduce, steal, kidnap and devour, a fanciful dreaming, the portrayal of the fine line that separates man from beast, and the perilous fall into that chasm of a most merciless existence.

"What you're perceiving, Larry, isn't real; nor are the rumours about you, even your existence.

You are a man lost behind a visual screen of thought. You have never once devoured a woman or a man. Never once have you kidnapped a child. And your wife, she, like you, has drifted facedown in this rivulet of fanciful horror for a long, long time."

Larry began then to look at his hands and he saw they were quite human and normal. He started to remember his life, and the many lives he'd forgotten.

"It is true, some of what they have whispered about. You are older than any living man. In fact, through your mental strength and the power of God, you reached a state of agelessness; not growing perceivably more in years than 33."

"How do you know all of this?" asked Larry.

"Because of an angel, one without wings. A moment ago he was hovering above your person, but I caught sight of him, and by his eyes I saw what has happened to you, or what you've allowed happen to yourself."

"Allowed to happen?"

"Yes. You might remember all before long, but the emergence of your frightful and entrancing-self began under the direction of the angel, whom we shall refer to as TOWU, in the first dark-age (or, Kali Yuga) known to this Island Universe on which we dwell.

"TOWU granted you power and your every desire, and cast you into a world of fantastical delirium; at the same time granting you the Ageless State."

"And what about my Queen, the Primordial Womb, the Moons, the Spine in the sands, the Priestesses, all of this?"

"It is a strong dream, nothing more. But the question is, Larry, do you want it to continue or do you want to wake up?"

Larry became thoughtful for a while, and then he gave his old, mischievous toothy grin, and he grew tall, and his body throbbed with the ethereal strength he was so accustomed to, and, unseen by the eyes around (other than for Nigel's), Larry the Lizard, in one long breath, hissed: *"Why would I do that when I have all this power?"* And he slashed one claw through the air toward Nigel, whose flustered purple face disappeared as a Great Shadow came over him and breathed him head-to-toe into the earth (a breath of dark wind falling away under Larry's terrible claw).

#

Over the scene whence the Queen (out of the sewers and onto the streets of Maya) of Larry's kind had emerged, high and lofty winds fell from the sky as Larry refused to relinquish the delirium of his power.

"But Larry, you are meant for greater things," Nigel tried to explain, "however you were disallowed, your unrequited love, self-loathing, you must let this go. The Lust Demon mustn't infect you; mustn't harden anymore your heart. And the people mustn't be mesmerised by your *charm* any longer; you're meant for greater things." Larry tilted his head at this and questioned Nigel with the swirling yellows of his eyes.

"You see, Larry, your rampant desire is unwholesome, but there's a reason you've so strong an impulse: Heaven.

"It's not that you're evil. This world is a test; God wants to try your strength, and see which side of yourself you choose, the good or the bad."

"And what is bad?"

"Let me show you."

Whilst the procession continued around the streets of Maya, Nigel and Larry departed to visit old haunts and memories. "Up there?" asked Larry, the green luminance of his scales coruscating for a moment.

"Yes," said Nigel, seeing the man beneath the astral figure of Larry, a man of average height with a scruffy beard, not a towering lizard of inscrutable nature; and in his blue eyes Nigel saw something meek and indifferent: human.

"But my wife was murdered," smiled that great lizard and hissed he through those swirling eyes.

"On me, Larry," said Nigel as he opened the front doors to the grey block of apartments that held once the penthouse abode of Larry's wife. Up the tall, winding steps they trod. Into the dingy apartment of a muddy-brown wallpaper and slimy-green carpet. The walls seemed vast when they entered, a great mire one could sink through if improperly touched. "Go to her," urged Nigel to Larry. "They have not taken her, for none can see her." And Larry did as Nigel bade, albeit with a glowering to his eyes, and he saw her: the closed oyster.—Only this time it was not foul with her venomous reek but instead cleanly-smelling and tempered with a memory; and when Larry touched the stone of her deceased fleshed, he was filled with a vision....

Three children with ginger hair (one girl and two boys) jumped on the sofa and kicked at the air, laughing gaily as a woman with shinning, long blonde hair cooked and cleaned and slaved away so that their small home was well-nourished and a man (her husband) in a grey suit could relax when from work he arrived home. But he did not relax. He walked through the apartment door without any cheer and scowled at the playful children, and would not kiss his wife, for he stank of the other women all day that he had seduced; as a salesman might.

"Why won't you kiss Mummy?" asked the little girl with a short-temper. Her father scowled and grew red. The two boys began to charge around the apartment with their ginger heads, like small Minotaurs. Their father stood up and shouted at them, "Stop it! You'll hurt yourselves!" And then they did, but it was by way of consequence, because, when the boys galloped into their father, he picked them up and threw them out the open kitchen window. The girl began to scream, "Mummy! Mummy!" and shake her ginger locks, angrily; yet before their mother could appear, the father chucked his little girl out the window also!

"What's going on?" asked the mother to her husband when she was done adorning herself with precious trinkets and painting her face in pleasing, lustrous colours. "Where are the children?"

"They've gone outside to play," answered the husband.

"Mummy! Mummy!" came three small voices in chorus up to the kitchen window. Their mother looked out the window and saw her children jumping on the canopy behind their block of apartments; "Get off there," cried their mother to them, "that is not ours and belongs to the hotel next door."

"But Daddy threw us out the window!" the children hollered up.

"What what what!" yelled the mother at the father.

"They wouldn't behave, dear."

"So you threw them out the window? Do you have any idea how far down that is?"

"Not the slightest, dear," said the husband nonchalantly.

"You animal," wept the mother as she ran out the apartment to fetch the children.

At the time the father had not thought on it very much, and that's not so bad (because thinking can hurt your head at times). But as Larry witnessed this vision he wished for a better nature; and it took Nigel to step in and say: "When the lizard appears over you, be ready to fight him with the Sword of Resting Stillness."

#

Soon enough, Larry found himself wanting to visit that room of darkness and its lambent mist and twinkling stars (the Room of Glimmering), and to sit by the willow and dark waters, to contemplate. And as he did this, a beautiful creature with strangely wide, spanning wings and ivory teeth and golden eyes emerged out of the waters and disturbed Larry as he sat under the blue-leaf vines. At first, Larry had his eyes closed, and felt but the water fleck his face and neck, and then a Shadow seemed to eclipse him and he opened his eyes and what he saw baffled and amused him; for, like himself, a man whom projected a fanciful creature atop his person could be seen striding through the air toward Larry, and as this man did so, the winged, ethereal creature of golden eyes and ivory teeth dissipated and a man with brown eyes and brown hair met Larry and sat down beside him and talked at length about the Room of Glimmering to he.

After much discourse, Larry finally began to ask questions, and the responses from his visitor painted a tale of a great struggle against a Shadow and Dragon which had impersonated him and driven him mad with both curiosity and fear. The visitor told Larry that he had once dwelt upon the Surface as an ordinary man, until the woe of his true love's passing. He beguiled a Goddess to take him to that Path of Bone Larry knows too well, and under the green Primordial Moon he brought his love back from the dead.

Unfortunately, the Goddess grew extremely jealous and dragged both of them under the blue Primordial Moon and cast them into a prison within the man's mind. "The Queen saved me from the delusion of that prison," the visitor told Larry. "Anyway, I must go now. It has been most pleasant talking to you here. I hope we meet again." And like that, the man whom had glided down and strolled through the air to sit beside Larry was gone.

PART II

Purple became the sky over Maya Metropolis as the Detective Inspectors (under the direction of S. N. A. K. E.) continued to search for a way to breach that underworld of Larry's kind. And the Queen grew and grew in beauty and size until dwarfed She the Metropolis like a man over an ant hill; and blotted She the sun from the sky with Her smiling, glowing face.

All but Nigel was tantalised and endeared by Her towering beauty reaching now up to the heavens. All but Nigel worked in the direction the Queen so desired. Nigel, with his Catus Felis, communicated with the Authoritarian Strongholds, writing letters about what he had witnessed, making phone calls, demanding that the King put a stop to the parlour tricks of their invader, Her Majesty. (But the King would do no such thing.)

"The green-skinned man is a friend," told Larry to Nigel. "You needn't mind his arrows. Beauty is as beauty seems." Nigel had been struggling with the vision of the Queen his eyes had seen and hands felt, and when Larry told him this, Nigel struggled less, and quite immediately.

Beauty is as beauty seems, thought Nigel to himself. "I understand…" said Nigel to Larry. They were back in Larry's office, and after Larry spoke these words to Nigel, Nigel began taking down the yellow tape, and he to himself continued to narrate: *Beauty is as beauty seems, beauty is as beauty seems, beauty is as beauty seems.*

Shortly after this, Nigel was pricked with one of the Queen's arrows. And instead of writing letters about Her parlour tricks, and the need to put a stop to Her, he wrote poetry to express Her beauty in line and verse.

The Queen began to lament over the Metropolis, and dark clouds gathered about Her head, and She wept and wept until, by Her lamenting and tears, all that was filthy and had come up from out of sewers was washed away. The gruff-bearded man with blue eyes and a meek smile grew very happy at this, and he began to talk to the denizens of the Metropolis and to shake hands with them and to tell them that all will be well and that his Queen is good and cares greatly for them.

Nigel brushed past the citizens of Maya Metropolis crowded around the feet of the Queen, and he read a poem he had written which went like this:

"That tall, tall tree,
a silhouette of green in the sky,
oh, how high its vessel does fly
up in that blue, blue sky

"That tall, tall tree up in the sky,
where the wind blows
ever stronger than below,
how it has grown ever-so-high
to sail seas of sky-blue sky,
marking the blue with a permanent dye,
like an eyelash,

natural by Her blinking eye.

"That tall, tall building
up in the sky,
a dark-grey silhouette
in Her blue, blue eye,
unmoving, unyielding,
like it cannot die

"but the wind blows tall;
the wind blows low;
the wind blows all
under Her blue dome of sky.

"Unyielding, unmoving,
like it cannot die,
the wind blows all
under Her Blue Dome of sky

"Even the clouds, because it is fair,
even the birds, who will not despair,
all blow in the blue, blue air

"But like a dark silhouette,
like a shadow in Her eye,
like a dead pigment up high,
there is a stain in the sky

"That tall, tall building up in the sky,
how one day you will learn,
learn the dust,
climbing up, like a shadow, so marvellously high,

learn the dust;
learn the dust:
When she blinks Her mysterious blue eye.

"Unmoving, unyielding,
like it cannot die,
the wind blows all
under Her Blue Dome of sky."

Quite happy became the Queen at hearing this poem expounded by Nigel, the one denizen to have recoiled at Her in disgust, and, hearing the words of the poem, she withdrew the darkness from the clouds about her head, spun a platform made of white, fluffy cloud-stuff and plopped Nigel onto it by her hand; then she began to wave her hands over the buildings of Maya Metropolis and oak, rowan, willow and elm, crabapple and sycamore, maple and alder trees began to sprout out of the ground, between the tall buildings of the Metropolis and along the streets in an order so fetching to the eye that one's breath was immediately taken away, and a fresher breath of air given.

She smiled brilliantly upon the denizens far beneath her, and Her height became once more like theirs, and the air around the Metropolis was at once far cleaner and easier to breathe.

It wasn't long after this change in events that the King deigned to meet the Queen; and it was almost at once that She and He fell in love with one another and looked to join their Kingdoms in holy matrimony. The King, a rather small fellow with a crown made of copper, a thick orange moustache and a face that would never smile but always seemed on the brink of laughter, thanked Nigel warmly and promoted his rank within the Authoritarian Stronghold and made he also the new mayor of Maya Metropolis.

In the penthouse abode of Larry's deceased wife, Larry showered and shaved; Nigel was present, and from the living room asked when the last time was that Larry cleaned himself. Larry did not answer but gave a quiet disgruntled hiss. "Have you ever changed your suit? Or, even, washed it?" Nigel asked next. Again, Larry gave a disgruntled hiss. Looking through a wardrobe in the bedroom of the suite, Nigel pulled out a fresh suit of the same type from as many suits as could fit sensibly into a moderate wardrobe. He called, "Ive found you a clean one, ol' boy."

Larry did not hiss this time but appeared in the doorway of the bedroom, damp from showering, his face clean-shaven, his skin a slight pink. He smiled at Nigel and said, "Thank you," taking from him a clean suit. As for the suit covered in grime, Nigel absentmindedly put it down somewhere, forgetting its place almost immediately; and, unbeknownst to him, Larry the Lizard and his grimy suit disappeared from the penthouse abode, and the Surface World, leaving Nigel and *Larry the Man* behind.

#

Larry was sat beneath the red moon, cross-legged, his eyes closed. Ruby was with him, daughter and priestess of the Queen. She had loved him in the red

148

moon's light as her red eyes had seen into his and her red lips pressed against his lips; and he had been inside of her and they had commingled as one flesh, and Larry had bathed in beautiful shades of red until he felt pleasantly warm and secure in the glow of the red moon and the moon looked no longer so much like a gaping wound, and the black puddles about Larry had vanished, and the crying babes that resembled to him the sapling of his heart had gone, and all but Larry could hear was a gentle stir in the wind and the enchantment of Ruby's song. The Queen had requested Larry to sit beneath each one of the seven moon's and that he become still and take control of the illusions formed by they. And it was of his Queen that he thought as he searched for stillness within himself;

he was thinking of Her and the treasures and mysteries She had revealed to him within the many, shifting chambers and halls of Her abode.

Ill-lit was the room that Larry's mind in stillness to returned, he having recently found himself stumbling upon. A long, vast hall, bare and empty. In the distance of the hall he could feel his Queen's presence, and he saw there, beneath the orange glow of two sconces, a luminous figure draped in a long white gown. Larry walked the length of this vast hall to his Queen, and the white glow that had been about the outline of Her figure receded into the darkness as closer he became, and when he was behind Her, approaching from within the glare of torch flame, he saw that She radiated silver light and that all of Her figure was embellished and encapsulated in an orb of dazzling silver. She was not standing but sitting, although from afar She had appeared quite tall, and Her attention was not given to Larry when he arrived.

She was sat on a ledge of rough, dark-grey rock over a small pool, a semi-circle of dark, reflecting waters. Her right hand drifted across the surface of the water, and She sang softly; Her words were of a language Larry could not understand, but he felt his heart beating as though in rhythm to, and the beating of his heart seemed to excite him and then calm him, and he felt tranquilly detached from the heavy weight of his flesh and bones as his heart followed a melody that his Queen produced with her voice. Yet, She wasn't singing to Herself; it was to a man, and asleep he was, in the water of the pool.

Larry rounded then on the man in the pool and approached the left side of his Queen. He remained outside Her silver light, beneath the sconce flame, as he watched, and he gazed upon the man that to She sang as drifted She Her right hand over the surface of the water; Her shoulders faced Larry but Her head of long, golden hair was turned only toward this man, and Her purple eyes gazed into the dark reflection of the water. As She sang, Her silver light flickered with Her voice, delicately attune to Her words. Larry felt great joy laying eyes upon his Queen and seeing the mystery She was to him, his mind becoming absent from the great form of his flesh, from his flesh as a presence at all; but there was a subtle jealousy in the chamber of his heart, like a small and sharp lump of coal, and it pricked him when he gazed at the man the Queen caressed with Her song and Her silver, encapsulating glow, and Larry saw him and saw that he was handsome, and that he was no more than *mere human*; the water kissing gently as it swayed by the Queen's gentle touch the man's shoulders and neck, he looked in one glance as though he slept to this world, but in another he appeared to be awake, as it was that a faint restlessness seemed to writhe through his muscles and across his skin in slight, flickering movements, his eyelids shut tight yet seeming they forever on the verge of opening. He was caucasian. His face was both intelligent and kind, his cheekbones feminine and his jaw elegant and, without being *very* wide, masculine. His lips were as though of a perfect lover's, a serenader of women; his ears were well-formed and poked out only slightly from the sides of thick, shoulder-length brown hair; and Larry grew jealous as he beheld the man's details, and the sharp lump of coal in Larry's heart pricked and pierced the tranquil rhythm of his breath and the flow and steady pulse of his blood, and to the dense and angry feeling of flesh the calm of his spirit evaporated. The Queen looked up and to Her left. Her singing stopped; Her glow retreated; and She addressed Larry as their eyes made contact, and Her purple gaze dove into the swirling yellows of his restless stare, and She said: "Child, my love for you is as a thousand blossoming springs; fare not the suffering of jealousy, or anger, for these things but *mask* the soul and *bind* you to your flesh."

Her gaze fell then upon the man in the pool, and She stroked his shoulder-length brown hair with a mother's touch, and She said, Her voice hovering over the pool of dark, reflecting water, "This man, this poor, poor man. He came from a Surface above. He is sustained by the pool's water, as indefinitely as I can hold him; for a war wages over the Land of his Soul: a world contained within the boundaries of his perpetrated mind.

"He came with a Goddess. He had wooed her high-above, on one of the Surface Worlds. And he told her that he wished to gaze upon the Primordial Moons with her. But it was a trick; for he needed the accompaniment and guidance of a Goddess to travel to our world, as he sought the moons of this land with dire hope: a hope to bring back love from beyond the grave. He had learnt in ancient texts of this world, and had read and thoroughly acquainted himself with the magics of the astral; fancied he that it could work; and it did.

"Though his tale still continues, he having met tragic and horrifying turns in plot—for *the rebuke of the Goddess*. She was most vengeful when she learnt of his real intention, and when she saw him with his lover revived, them together, under the green moon, where he had so brought his love back from the astral realms of the dead, the Goddess dragged them into the air; and she flew them beneath the blue moon, and by the blue moon's light, she cast a great trickery over the man. The moons are powerful. The moons can see all things. They craft illusions to lure you from the narrow path, and upon venturing from the Path of Bone, it is near impossible to find a way back; and when the power of a Goddess beams bright and a moon's rays are woven together by the deeds of her heart, a power is summoned from the Underworlds, a great will of power; and so it was the man and his lover were torn apart, trapped on the opposite sides of a world contained within his very mind.

"It was under the blue moon that I found him. I felt a great disturbance in my creatures and the night outside and I set out to see what had happened, and when I entered into the blue light, the Path vanished beneath me. And I was in a great and terrible wood. A woodland of deceptive shadows and steep slopes. I found him at the back of a garden to the home he now believes is his, on the edge of an unfathomable woodland. It seems that she, the Goddess, has imprisoned him again and again upon each attempt he has made to conquer her. Haunted by a shadow that threatens to steal his form, his identity, driven mad he has travelled many times through the woodland aback his home, and he has found the land of his love, and has fought with the foul beast the Goddess has become; but the fight remains within himself, and whilst delusion has ahold and manipulates him with brief endings of happiness and love, and draws of his power, I cannot help him. But from time to time, I try. I do what I can."

She raised Her right hand over the man's sleeping, stirring face, and a golden light emitted from Her palm; and the pool, and Her white silken clad form, and the air, were all illuminated by the light of a brilliant, golden moth.

#

Larry lay beneath the orange moon with the daughters Ruby and Topaz. He lay, incapacitated, his vision filled with an hot, orange light. Ruby and Topaz, kneeled beside him. Ruby sang gently over Larry, and her voice afforded him some ease; his vision having first

153

gone black, until Ruby's voice washed over him, and Topaz kissed him and climbed on top of him. Larry's scaled body was tense, his heartbeat was both slow and hard, and his veins surged with a hot flow of blood, his flesh unbearably filled with the poison-honey of lust. He could not move but gaze upward, listening to Ruby's gentle voice, as Topaz climbed atop of him and her breasts came low to his face. Her orange eyes met with his and again she kissed him; and then he entered her; she embraced his phallus with the warmth and moisture between her thighs, and as Larry felt the length of his hardened member grow warm, entering deep into Topaz, her eyes ever glaring into the yellows of his, she breathing in the air that he breathed out, he breathing in hers; the suffocation of the orange moon's heat lessened, and the unbearable, slow pulse of lust that had turned his body ridged and stiff began to flow naturally through his body and leave him. And in that great comfort and release, as Ruby sang in a language that his ears did not comprehend but to his heart responded, and Topaz gazed with the bright orange hues of her eyes into his, Larry deep and throbbing in the wet warmth between her thighs, the orange moon beaming over him like both a passionate light and a blinding glare, Larry's vision and mind drifted from the enchantment of the Queen's daughters, and again he found himself wandering through the chambers of Her abode.

#

Stone steps were cold on his feet as he climbed a tall tower. Darkness was above and beneath him. Larry

154

leaped up the winding staircase, that only moments ago he had been at the bottom of, his claws running smoothly along the stone walls as he ascended. It was not long before he reached the end of the spiralling staircase and a pale, wooden door, though very high he had climbed.

He entered through the door of which there had been no handle to turn. He had pushed it forward and it had fallen into a crevice in the floor. He then had slid the door to the left and in he walked to a dimly lit belfry. A glass window ran along stone walls, encircling the room and allowing for a full view of the the Queen's castle beneath, the great crag Her lair behind dwelt, and the lands around. A dark moon shone brightly into the belfry and illuminated all surfaces therein with a black light. An amber flare glazed across the dark light of the room, however, lending fiery hue to the illuminated darkness, for the presence of the city that sat in clouds beneath the black light of a dark moon, the city that whirred with noise, and of bright, artificial lights; Maya Metropolis.

In the centre of the belfry Larry stood and beneath him was a glass floor, a symbol made of blue and encircled by a metal band of gold, and in the centre, where Larry stood, *beneath his feet*, a white, five-pointed star. Above his head was a bell absent any ringing mechanism, absent a clapper within the sound bow; a rope extended down in a corner of the room, but Larry did not think that the bell should work, and it puzzled him. He was standing tall, his height unfurled, his head close to the sound bow of the bell, when the Queen appeared behind him and the room lit up in a soft white glow.

Larry didn't mind the surprise. He liked it when someone or something surprised him. He liked it even more when that someone was the Queen. He bent and crouched low, as to be of similar height to the Queen. Her purple eyes gazed upwards, Larry peering down, his green, scaled body between him and Her. Her amethyst crown shone, brightly and purple, for the white glow she exuded, seven sky-blue pearls glimmering atop seats of the crown. Larry couldn't help but notice the bare skin of Her chest showing through a parting in her silken gown, and that she was cold and goosebumps ran along Her skin, and Her nipples stood erect beneath the white silken cloth of her dress. Her purple lips began to form words and Larry bent lower, gazing into his Queen's eyes, his yellow gaze swirling.

"You have a great journey ahead of you yet, Larry. This room will serve you in that journey one day, and the bell above your head will ring and you will hear its music." Her lips glistened in the dark light of the moon and Her form dripped with the fiery hue of artificial lights from the city in clouds. Larry was almost level with Her now, his eyes, his yellow Lizard eyes wide and gazing into Her benign purple stare; She had spoken so softly to him, he felt almost that She had intended to seduce him. But it was not the case. Larry had not seen the Queen for some days, and whilst Her daughters satisfied him, it was always Her that he had wanted; Her precious milk, not theirs, that he desired to taste; Her lips pressing against the hard scales of his body, not the seven lips of Her daughters, as satisfying as he found their company; the Queen reached with Her right hand and felt Larry's smiling, scaled countenance, and She kissed him, Her purple lips pressed to his, and Larry grabbed Her. His claws wrapped around the small of Her back and he pulled his Queen close to him, Her wings suddenly unfurling beneath the long strands of Her golden hair.

The Queen did not struggle at Larry's quick embrace. She but continued to kiss him. And Larry grew with great excitement as Her lips pressed against his scales and Her breasts rubbed against him. With his left claw he then pulled the silken gown from her shoulders and it dropped to the floor beneath as he then lift Her into the air. She radiated with a soothing heat that nourished, but Larry burned with passion, and his phallus had grown long between his legs and grown hard. It was in this moment that he ravaged Her, that he lost control and the Queen's majesty, Her motherly quarter, was lost behind the dark fires of desire.

He lowered Her naked body, holding Her gently by Her shoulders, bringing Her face level with his groin, his phallus sliding along Her flesh until level it became with Her soft, purple gaze. And gently, he pushed the head of his hardened member toward Her mouth, and Her lips parted, and Larry forced himself deep into Her throat. Her body had hung limp the second he'd lowered Her and then pushed himself inside Her mouth. Her lips had cease to kiss. Warmth had left Her flesh, and Her eyes shut tight. But Larry continued to thrust with his phallus into the slippery tightness of Her throat, Her purple lips sliding across him as he pleased hisself.

The Queen's white glow was not any longer of Her. Her gown lay on the floor under Her, like a snake's dead skin, Her golden hair reaching as far down as to touch its cloth. It was as Larry filled her throat with his seed that Her eyes reopened, and Larry, not stopping in his action toward his Queen, was struck by a blinding whiteness as She peered up at him, and Her hands laid on his flesh, Her touch claiming his energies, and She slid her lips along the shaft of his phallus, slowly, tenderly, until it was only the head of his male member that was placed in Her mouth, and She continued then to slide Her lips across his excited flesh until His heart became very slow and all his fervour left him; his phallus growing then small as the Queen removed Her mouth and kissed the shrinking head of his snake with wet, purple lips. Larry became weakened, and he placed his Queen on the floor.

Already was she dressed in her gown when he looked up. Leaning against a wall of the belfry, unable to stand, he saw his Queen upon the five pointed star, Her wings spanning the room and ablaze with a fiery hue, and the room became flooded with blue light that formed beneath Her feet, and Her figure before him pulsed and shimmered with a white glow as five points of light pulsated from the centre of Her mass, and Larry was pressed against the wall that he leant on by an expanding band of gold metal; and Her voice rung over the room:

"Your journey will begin when your sons are born, and you expose yourself to the rebuke of my daughters."

#

Ruby, Topaz and Sunstone stood on the Path of Bone, ahead of Larry. Each were they clad in black satin dresses and each were they busy casting with their lips as they trod apprehensively backward, stumbling and tripping upon the wide tails of their gowns that fell upon the earth like a magician's cloth and hid from sight the narrow path, an enchantment to subdue the transformation of a one *not* so happy and smiling Larry. Beneath a moon of yellow fire and cool heat, with tongues of blue flame like petals waving against a background of sky, Larry looked to the earth beneath, to flame having risen under his feet; yellow astral flames projecting a great heat into his flesh, his chest heaving with the will of a sun therein contained; and a great confusion in his mind unearthed itself, a great tension and pain; the Queen was pregnant with his sons, and there was a glimmer in Her eyes, like a reckoning, a bright judgement in Her right eye, and an impaling darkness to Her left.

Larry had grown sick beneath the yellow moon this time, having he bounded past it and contemplated plucking the fiery yellow mass from the sky and giving it to his Queen as a gift last he passed under it; his blood had turned dark and his left side venomous with rage; his right flooding with a will to restrain the surging anger. Sunstone's eyes glimmered from afar upon the Path of Bone where astral fires had not risen; and Larry had two thoughts to his mind: the first, that the absence of flames might halt his continual growth and remove the venom beating through the channel of his left being and heart; the second, that he would pummel those who dared to cast a spell over him, and that Sunstone's bright gem-like eyes would make an excellent gift to Her Majesty.

Larry lumbered forward with far reaching strides. Confronted by two wills, he was restrained in his speed, his movements an unclean lurching; the left side of him was darkened by the presence of purple veins and black patches growing quickly across his flesh; his right arm seemed to swing across his body in an attempt to injure his left leg already walking with an irregularly crook in the knee; truly, Larry was a fearsome spectacle, a deadly offender, his shoulders themselves reaching into the sky, but if one saw this from afar, they would surely stare and be quite puzzled; perhaps terror would be an overconfident verdict to suggest, perhaps not.

As Sunstone's eyes glimmered and flashed like sharp, yellow beams of light from afar, Larry's contorted mind was thrown backward into the recollection of past events, and he found hisself in his Queen's throne room, She sat on Her oyster throne, Her belly gravid, all of Her subjects stood in waiting as Larry barged into the golden hall of pink, seductive ambiance and scent.

Larry's last visit with the Queen was buried in a dark chamber of remembrance; he had not seen Her since then for three times the length of Her prior absence. What he did remember of their encounter in the belfry where last they met, most pungently within his mind, were Her words, and the crushing band of gold that had pinned him with such ease and triumph against the walls of the belfry. And it was then, where his memory now returned, and that just as he opened a door in the Queen's shifting lair, unpredictably, the chamber which happened to appear before him and that he walked into was Her throne room, and at first he did not notice this, for in the moment his clawed, scaled hand pressed against the door in the belfry, his inner vision flashed with Her white glow and two purple dots stared and hovered from within a distance of his mind, and Her words breathed through his ears: "*Your journey will begin when your sons are born, and you expose yourself to the rebuke of my daughters.*"

White glow evaporating from his mind, Larry was met by the intoxication of pink light and a perfumed scent filled his lungs; in the distance, upon a throne, two purple dots, glimmering eyes, stared across the hall and lovingly met with his confused, disoriented gaze.

The white carpet was beneath his feet and lining the walls were the lizards of the Queen, three rows of them along each wall, and Her daughters stood before him, their gowns of black satin displaying wide and frivolous tails. There was an atmosphere of the hall that Larry did not recall when last he had entered, when first he had arrived. All eyes seemed to have been awaiting him, and they glimmered with a joy and appraisal, each eye, of lizard, of daughter, and Larry was pushed forward by an urgency born off the sincerity of each glimmer that met with his eyes. The Queen's daughters parted and Larry passed them, theirs smiles following him down the white carpet. Atop the Queen's pink oyster throne sat the Queen's owl, though this time it did not sleep, it peered at Larry as he approached Her Majesty, its eyes a magma-orange glare hot like fire on Larry's throat and chest.

Saw then he his Queen, and the roundness of Her belly, the fullness of life in her cheeks and the glow that emitted about Her flesh. Her bosom brimmed the top of her gown, and Larry saw that she was indeed pregnant, and again Her words reiterated theirselves in his mind; "*Your journey begins when your sons are born,*" and Larry bent on one knee and lowered his head, and offered the Queen his fealty, raising then his right hand with an upturned palm. The Queen stroked his palmar and She stood and She raised him to his feet. She moved with great ease in guiding him then down the steps away from Her throne. The owl lifted up into the air and swooped close past Larry's head and landed with gently clutching talons upon the Queen's shoulder.

Half way down the white carpet the Queen turned to Larry and whispered into his left ear: "Our sons will arrive tonight, my daughter's will escort you to their birthing waters." As Larry then noticed his feet over a black fissure of obsidian glass in the golden floor of the hall, the air about him filled with an ascending darkness and all figures, including the Queen and Her owl, disappeared, and Larry found himself plummeting and falling through darkness until a crescent moon's light illuminated his eyes.

With white, pale moonlight upon him Larry found that his scales glimmered and he felt suddenly joyful. At his feet then he noticed the silver mass of a hare. The hare looked up at him, wiggling black whiskers and pink nose, and with black eyes it asked him to follow, and it turned its shinning hide and hopped away into darkness and moonlight. Larry followed the hare, and around and around he went, dizzyingly, an illuminated darkness that through he could not see ahead but for the shinning fur of the hare; until a pool of water shimmered, that is, in a darkness in some far off angle, and the enclosing dark parted from his sides as he stepped into the scene of his sons' birthing. The hare had vanished and where Larry thought he had seen hop last its silver, shinning hide, his eyes found the black satin dresses of the Queen's seven daughters.

The seven daughters stood around an edge of the rocky earth wherein lapsed the water whereby Larry's sons were to be born—and there the Queen bathed beneath the red and orange, yellow, green, blue and purple gazes of Her daughters, and a crescent moon's silken light, silver as it is rays danced and hopped, reflected across the surface of the birthing pool, all light thus the Queen also bathed by. Her skin was pale, as ever it was, but the life usually seen in her cheeks, and the glow about her flesh, was absent Her, and truly pale did she look atop the dark waters of the birthing pool.

Larry approached the pool and the Queen's daughter Emerald stepped aside that he might stand before the Queen, and he saw then the hideousness that had become of Her flesh; the paleness that gave dark veins appearance. Her pulse was noticeable as spasmodic waves of dark-blood flowed through a beating vein in Her temple, and then in an instant it was not dark, for Her body beamed a gentle white, and for the moment that the wave of Her pulse changed, Her flesh beamed with life and a channel of light descended from the heavens as tho She were an actor upon a stage; and then again Her flesh became pale and hideousness was Her reek as black blood surged through dark veins. Continually did the Queen grow pale and moan with pain as darkness surged through Her veins; continually did Her flesh beam, intermittent to the darkness and hideousness that had come over Her; and atop the pool of birthing waters, beneath the silken stream of a crescent moon and the myriad colours of Her daughter's eyes, She began to give birth; the first moans that beset Her upon the birthing sang from Her lungs as dire pain, and three blood-red leaves of a great willow tree that sat perched on the opposite side of the birthing pool (its many roots buried in the rocky earth and extending into the birthing waters) glided past Larry's eyes, and each they fell upon the Queen and into the dark waters of the birthing pool became they submerged.

The vines of the willow swayed then, and a wind breathed through them, and the air grew wet with moisture, and the sky heaved and heaved above with continuous breaths, and it was as though the night cried as the Queen wailed and dark blood wrought Her flesh, and the moon's light failed, and the beams of Her daughters eyes shut, and by the yellow torches of Larry's vision was the first birth seeable;

as though it were she had given birth to stone, a small body emerged, charcoal-grey skin covering its head, and it fell beneath the waters. The Queen ceased to wail. Larry dove his left claw after it, and out he pulled the first of babes, offspring of his loins.

PART III

Millenniums have passed since Larry the Lizard left 'Larry the Man' alone, up-high to the Surface World of Maya Metropolis; Kings have come and gone,

Detective Inspectors have retired and eventually found their final resting place; the Metropolis has grown taller and broader, a great harmony having the reins of advancement in one hand, and a total control of the denizens in the other.

Larry has traversed the Path of Bone, contemplating under the moons and sleeping with the Queen's seven daughters, Ruby, Topaz, Sunstone, Emerald, Sapphire, and the twins both by the name of Amethyst and conjoined at the waist are they. He has grown in strength, and achieved remarkable control over his physical and astral form; being able to change his shape and size from that of a small gecko to the towering height of a behemoth lizard in a few licks of a second. Though, his control came only once he had learnt to calm himself under each Primordial Moon and to master their illusions and the daughters of the Queen, so that their power became his, and his power could rightfully, *truly*, unfurl.

Forgotten are the rumours throughout Maya of a one happy, smiling Larry the Lizard who killed with unseen hands its pretty denizens; that aphrodisiac to the tongue; Larry the Man, however, has not forgotten him but quite simply moved on—awaiting his return. Once the fallout-whispering passed, and generations began to ebb, Larry the Man felt rather less insane, and, having no immediate family, the sting of time was blunted. He still wore his green lizard scales, and by that I mean he retained both youthfulness and strength; but the insanity was driven out, and millenniums ago.

The king of Maya Metropolis is still rather a short man with an orange moustache, wearing a copper crown, as are the characteristics passed down in the royal bloodline. And still there is an absence of a smile from his face, a laughter ever-threatening to open jaws wide in a belly full of chuckles.

…Of course, we cannot continue this story without first revisiting the birthing pool of Larry's sons. Like stone fell the first of his offspring into dark water, and like a lump of coal fell the second. The sky above heaved and heaved and then heaved no more; Larry pulled them out of the birthing waters, and rubbed their chests to start the breathing. One he named Madness, and the other Turmoil.

Madness looked as though his scales were made of stone, and Turmoil was but a dark lump of coal with eyes, nose, a mouth and tail. Larry used his son's to conquer his foes up high, once they were fully grown; having matured under the Primordial Moons with him; he thought himself unstoppable. Prematurely to Larry's rise from the Underworld, Maya ceased to be peaceful—instead the inhabitants of that fine Metropolis began to argue with one another, continually. Larry the Man, watching, unseen, keeping himself away from the rising clamour, maintaining a meditative state suggestive of death, awaited Larry the Lizard, whom, he knew, would surely try to posses him.

#

Under the purple moon our lizard friend ventured and found he the twins, Amethyst and Amethyst. They rebuked him for his deeds up high, for the great delusion he caused over Larry the Man and the Metropolis, and they made him make an unbreakable oath, to *swear* that no matter the size of his power and his own desires, that he would always do as the Queen wished.

Millenniums have passed since Her Majesty visited the Surface, and no marriage came about then between the kingdom of that fine and upstanding Metropolis and Her realm beneath many surfaces. Not all queen's have needed a king, but Her Majesty looked to join Her realm with a kingdom up high; and Larry would have to play parlay in snagging for his Queen a king, and then a kingdom.

EPILOGUE: THE OYSTER THRONE

"Hiska, hiska, hiska Pöunnaoudris, rustle the Underworlds and slither from beneath the fountain of the Hyrda in Antropasis. Wake the Lords of Turmoil and Madness; I summon their bones to take form up above, in the world wherein lies Maya Metropolis; and thou also, Pöunnaoudris, thou, my most beautiful hatchling, shall take form in scales and by sunlight sow havoc, throwing a great snare by which we shall *catch a King*; do this for your Queen, Pöunnaoudris, and She will reward you with a Pearl of the Heavens, allowing thee access across the Seven Realms, to plunder, devour, and enslave to your heart's content," spake the Queen of all lizard kind from upon her marvellous oyster throne. Before Her stood Her seven sensuous and beautiful daughters, about Her Her blood hounds, and gathered together were all Her lizards faithful to Her. "And thou, Larry, thou wilt put an end to what you have started up above."

Larry the lizard pressed forward out of a crowd of his kind, pushing by an elderly blue lizard with dark green eyes, and two orange lizards with hulking frames and overcast white eyes; slinking along the golden floors to his Queen, minding not to step on the volcanic glass that filled splinters and grooves and broke the gold of Her lair up (of which the interior was mostly made) with a cold, dark shimmering of black.

The Queen's perching owl fidgeted slightly atop the rim of Her throne; its black talons scratching quietly against the pink oyster shell. Larry trembled as he neared Her, Her beauty filling him with desire and admiration so that he would fall pitifully before Her had his Queen asked him to grovel, and She said to him, "My boy, go and do my biding." And Larry slid away from Her presence, brushing by all the lizard kind gathered before Her throne, moving he this way and that between them, as though he had to zigzag through them, passing every one of them before he found the back of the crowd and could slink toward the front doors of Her Majesty's formidable lair.

Larry looked back as he placed his feet on the Queen's Spine set across the land of Her enchantment, feeling Her castle shiver around him as he scurried through the cave-like entrance of the Queen's lair, and the sky outside wailed loudly; for the winds that blow between all worlds were chattering noisily, and Larry looked back before the front doors slid shut, and he saw

Her owl that sits atop Her pink oyster throne with its eyes, wide open, magma-orange, watching Larry as Larry slipped away to do his Queen's biding; to return to Maya Metropolis.

TO BE CONTINUED...